The Cryptkey

The Search for the Lost Keys

Vamsi Atluri

Table of Contents

Dedication

To my son, you keep the child in me alive and your creativity
is my inspiration.

Acknowledgments

Thank you from the bottom of my heart for all the support from family and friends.

Thank You, to my readers for taking the time to read my book. I hope you enjoy it.

About the Author

Vamsi ""V"" Atluri was born in New York City and now lives in Sunny Las Vegas, Nevada with his wife, child and 2 dogs.

Vamsi has been in Information Technology for 24yrs and throughout his life his creative side spoke to him. After many years of no action he finally decided to take action and bring to life his creative side to share with world.

1.

The Lost Key

Scott arrived at school, as he did every day of the week, and it started with what seemed like a bad movie…as it did every day.

"Hey, stop it, get off me. Why can't you guys just leave me alone," yelled Scott to the bullies pushing him around as he was making his way through the yellow and brown gates in front of the school. They were poorly maintained and had sharp rusted edges along the vertical sides as you walked through. Scott thought to himself while still being pushed around, "They really should paint and fix these fences before someone gets cut and needs a tetanus shot." At this point, he was so used to his mornings of abuse from the other children that his mind would wander to other things.

He yelled again, "You guys do this to me every morning!!!!" Scott already wanted to go home to his hideout on 238 Fillever Dr, Montville, NJ. The hideout was the attic above the top floor of his house, where he would spend his free time every day after school. It's where he felt safe and at peace. It wasn't a shabby place to hang out; his father had helped him clean it up and make it something that Scott would enjoy – Like a man cave, but for kids!!! He had a nice green beanbag that could seat 4 people, not that he had many friends. The cushion-filled seat was placed just under the dormer, so the sunlight would be plenty as he read his books and lost himself in his imagination. Off to the right, he had a desk cluttered with pliers, wrenches, scissors, wires, circuit boards, and just about anything a tinkerer would have. To the left of the desk – in front of the beanbag, he had a nice 50-inch LED TV wired up to his PS5, Nintendo Switch, and Xbox. Sometimes he would game for hours on end, losing track of time and space altogether.

Scott's parents, Mr. John and Mrs. Sarah Hooper were simple and loving people who'd go to church every Sunday, volunteer for community work, and loved Scott very much. They encouraged him in all things he was interested in and supported him through all his ups and downs.

Mr. Hooper was a banker in a bank called Fannings. He was a tall, slender man with a long neck and sculpted muscles. Mrs. Hooper was a beautiful brunette who loved wearing dresses, gardening in her free time, and making quick trips to the farmer's market to buy ingredients for her favorite shepherd's pie. The Hoopers had two children; Miranda, a 16-year-old, who Scott felt was the favorite of the two but also knew he was loved just as much. They also had a dog named Zero, who they named after a dog they saw in a movie.

Every morning, Mrs. Hooper would wake up at 6 am sharp, wear her favorite yellow apron, and make breakfast for the entire family. Then, an hour later, Mr. Hooper would come out of his room, give Mrs. Hooper a peck on the forehead, and sit in front of the television, catching up on the morning news.

"Miranda…Scott, honey, you have school in an hour. Hurry up. Breakfast is ready." Mrs. Hooper would scream from the kitchen.

Each day she'd set the table with the most perfectly cooked sunny side-ups, some pancakes, juice for the kids, coffee for the adults, freshly cut fruits, and some bread. Life was perfect; until Scott had to go to school in the morning.

While the rest of the Hoopers lived a perfect life with nothing too out of the ordinary, things were different for Scott Hooper. Scott was born with a gift that set him apart from the rest of his family - he was a special child. While most kids grow up exploring their imaginations, Scott constantly tinkered with gadgets, taking electronics apart and rebuilding them into something entirely different. One time, he built a radio that could pick up signals all the way from Europe. At times he battled against dark thoughts resulting from the daily bullying, and his imagination and ingenuity was the only thing that kept him in the light.

The other children in school quickly learned to stay away from him, as even simple conversations were difficult to have, as Scott's mind would wander off onto some project he was either thinking of or working on or to some distant place where his imagination would take him. Scott tried hard to adjust and fit in like everyone else, but it just wasn't working out for him. He would go home after school with black eyes, bloody noses, and the smell of dirt and sweat permeating his clothes and hair. This only made it worse when he returned to school the next day looking like a walking zombie from tinkering all night and his face and body all bruised up, much to his mother's dismay. Eventually, Scott started skipping school so often that he had to go to court for truancy. He was sentenced to community service at the local library, where he spent most of his days sitting in the corner alone, reading books, and drinking soda pop all day long.

One weekend, Scott had worked hard, all night and day, for a presentation due on a Monday. When the day came for him to present, the usual bullies somehow sabotaged his presentation by removing some parts that Scott did not notice. As he started to turn on the device he had created by touching the fingerprint reader on the side, it began to smoke and spark, almost catching fire. Scott yelled, "What the heck! This was working this morning when I tested it." He was in tears, as this caused Scott immense humiliation and embarrassment in the classroom. It was supposed to turn on and show various audible frequencies in the air between 2 antennas and different colors, depending on the pitch of the sound. Not to mention, the teacher also graded him badly, which took a toll on him. The entire class laughed at Scott and bullied him for messing up the project.

In the act of sheer embarrassment and hurt, Scott fled the premises, ran to the school playground, and hid under the bleachers, with no plans to go back for the 2nd-period class. Finally, after the 3rd period, the principal found him sleeping under the shade and called Mrs. Hooper.

The principal explained to Mrs.Hooper that he had been doing this often; skipping classes and hiding in different parts of the school. Mrs.Hooper responded with anger and pain in her voice, "But don't you see. My son is constantly being bullied at school. Why doesn't the school do anything about it?" Mrs. Hooper argued with the principal as Scott waited in the hallway.

"We have already provided Scott with a counselor, Mrs. Hooper, but your child refuses to see him. We can't force him!!!"

"Why can't you do something about the bullies? This isn't the first time this has happened!!! Suspend or expel those kids. You are the principal."

"Scott started it, Mrs. Hooper. Look, we're trying our best to accommodate the child at our school," said the principal as she took out a pamphlet from her desk's bottom-right drawer. "I'd like you to visit these schools. Scott is a special child, and I believe he deserves a school with more advanced teachers and students who would understand him better," she added.

"My son does not start fights; you can't possibly be....." started Mrs. Hooper.

"...Just take them, please," said the principal forcing the pamphlets into Mrs. Hooper's hands. "You and I both want the best for Scott," she added.

On her way home, Mrs. Hooper silently drove, wondering what she would tell Mr. Hooper at dinner tonight, while Scott sat in the passenger seat, quietly looking outside the window.

When they arrived home, Scott darted toward his room before his mother could even say something. She let him be for the rest of the evening while she prepped dinner.

It's not that he was bad-looking, but his ability to make himself look like an outcast allowed others to exploit him. He was quiet but not out of shyness. Most of the time, he was living in another world in his mind. He was a reserved boy, as if it were a conscious choice to the lie of the land before he got involved. However, he was never stand-offish; he distanced himself from everyone and spent all his time reading books or walking Zero. You'd never see Scott go out or make friends deliberately. Nothing was threatening about him. Scott was a great listener and an A-grade student who had never failed a class. Once in a while, he would sulk over not getting his schoolwork right and had poor tolerance about it.

At dinner, the kids ate their food in silence while Mrs. Hopper narrated her day's events to Mr. Hooper. Even Miranda had things to talk about, but Scott sat and patiently listened while his parents discussed changing schools. Once dinner was done, Scott went to his room immediately.

He was furious. "Why do I have to change?" he asked himself that night as he lay awake in bed. "I am perfectly happy here," he said out loud as he ran his hand through his hair, "and I'm not changing anything."

"I know, Scott," his father answered from the doorway, "but I've heard you say this before, and your mother and I agreed it's better to move than to be unhappy or dissatisfied all the time."

Hurt, Scott turned in bed to face the wall and hide his tears from his father. He lay still in the same position for the next hour until everyone had gone to bed and the lights were turned off. It was past his curfew, but he needed some fresh air. Scott put on his trunks and put a leash on Zero. The two best friends headed for the park in the night's silent hours. The moonlight made shadows dance around them, and they walked slowly through the darkness surrounding them like a shroud of death, hiding secrets they could not begin to understand yet, but would never forget in their lifetimes. As they neared the park, they noticed something peculiar: no one else was there, not even a single car or truck to be seen. The streetlights were all dark, and no sounds of people coming and going were heard except for the soft sound of the wind, rustling leaves, and trees, as if trying to warn them of danger ahead.

They continued until they came upon a small pond in the center of a circular driveway with a large fountain at the edge. It was dry and appeared to have been there for years, although it didn't look like any water had ever flowed through it. It looked as though someone had removed it from its moorings long ago and placed it back in this spot without knowing how to get it back up and running again; so it wouldn't leak into the surrounding land or the area around it. Scott thought it was placed there to keep it out of sight.

A bit further past the circular driveway and oddly-placed fountain, he was near the park right next to a construction site, normally busy with workers during the day. However, it was so silent at this hour that you could hear a feather drop. Today, Scott felt a little adventurous and decided to explore a bit more, so he headed toward the construction site. He arrived and saw several dump trucks parked on one side; no men were in sight. No one would be there until morning, and it was going to be a long, long night for Scott and Zero. So, Scott took advantage of the silence and quietly climbed into one of the dump trucks. In his head, he was imagining workers coming back to the site and himself jumping out onto the ground and running to the nearest building to hide. While he drafted the heroic scene in his mind, he realized he had let go of Zero's leash, and the dog was wandering on its own.

Panicking, Scott rushed toward Zero, who was happily rolling over in a muddy puddle.

"Come on, boy!" Scott said, annoyed.

But the deed was done. Zero now lay covered in mud; there was nothing Scott could do about it. So he gave up and sat next to the dog, watching him have a great time.

A few minutes later, when the two were about to make their way back home, Scott tripped on a metal beam and rolled head-first into a pit dug by the construction workers. He bumped his head pretty hard, but to his surprise, it didn't hurt. When his head hit the ground, he heard a hollow sound, the sound your head would make had you hit a tin or something hollow. He started to dig around that area, and as his hands started to touch what seemed to be a rectangular object, it started to glow, a light so bright that it was almost blinding. Zero began barking at the light too. It seemed as though, Zero was as curious about the object as Scott was. The two began to dig together, finally uncovering the object in its entirety.

"What is that?" Scott exclaimed, "I don't know if I should open it…"

Zero continued his barking, and soon both of them were kneeling in front of the box, examining its exterior. It felt like the box whispered of unspoken adventure in its subdued sweet browns, the lid inviting its opening. Scott looked around to see if anyone was around him, whispering in his ears. Either way, it was the adventure that sought him.

Carefully, Scott picked up the box and held it in his hands. He ran his fingers through the letters and shapes carved onto the box. He could not make anything of the foreign language, and he felt a sharp pain in his head as he tried to decipher what the words meant. The box was very old and made from some material that looked like it had been reclaimed from a shipwreck or some sort of shipbuilding project centuries ago, but it still stood firm today. However, it had a few interesting features that were kind of alien but also looked like butterflies made of a strong and shiny metal underneath it.

Gradually, Scott kept the box back on the ground and waited for something to change, anything. A few minutes passed, and nothing happened; it still continued to glow, so he decided to open the box and see what its contents revealed.

As Scott lifted the lid of the box, in it lay what seemed like a circular object, covered in some dirt that seemed to have gotten in from its surroundings. But upon looking closer, it was shaped like a hexagon, but not a normal hexagon. At every part that was supposed to be flat, it bent down, then flat again with sharp points at each outer-intersecting corner. The key resembled the ornate top of olden days craftsmanship. There was something magical about it – like an epiphany in a void, bringing forth a revelation to whoever held the object. On it were some engravings, which looked like nothing he had ever seen. Scott carefully picked up the object in his delicate fingers, metal, and skin together. There was a strange warmth to it, and the faded moonlight played gently over its edges. He slowly curled his fingers around it. Feeling some strange energy emitting from it into his body, making all the little hairs on his body stand up and dance.

Scott turned the object over in his hands; the metallic side glistening in all its glory, faced him. His heart was beating faster by the minute, and Zero now lay silently beside him. As he brushed off the dust from each of the edges of the object, he pricked his finger, causing him to bleed.

Scott was blinded by a sudden bright light that took over most of the property. It was the kind of brightness that engulfed you in it, and there was no escaping it. He felt his body tingle with indescribable sensations, almost like pins and needles were pinching him from head to toe. His skin was being stretched like he was being torn apart, limb by limb, and put back together repeatedly. It wasn't painful, and it only lasted a few moments.

2.

Scarsova

'Bam!' Scott landed with a thud on a dry piece of land, as arid as the Sahara.

'Ahh!' he grabbed his head in his hands as if gripping tightly would subside the now stinging pain. As he slowly tried to put the weight of his body on his feeble knees, Scott realized Zero was not by his side.

Scott panicked and screamed for his dog. "Zero....Zero come here, boy..." he tried to yell. The bones in his body felt like they were being crushed all at once, and there was only so much sound he could mutter from his aching lungs.

He tried to stand on his feet but was unable to when he realized he was no longer at the construction site. Scott looked around to see a familiar face or a clue as to where he was, but it all felt so strange.

"What just happened, where... where am I, where is Zero?" Scott asked as he lay there on the ground, his body slowly starting to feel normal. He remembered finding a key at the site, and then it all went black, and he fell into this strange land.

Finally able to get to his feet, he wandered carefully ahead and noticed a blanket of rocks scattered with sparse spots of whites and yellows. The air he inhaled had a sharp, salty, tingling feeling, with something reflecting off it as if colorful bright hues were dropped into the current of air with precision. He felt cold; even though this strange place resembled that of a hot desert, it was freezing. The silence eddied around his body eerily.

'Hello…is anybody here?' Scott yelled. His teeth were jittering from the cold. It was dead-silent as if sound waves could not travel here; he could barely even hear his own echo back. Suddenly, bright lights flickered across the vast darkness of space.

There was a sudden movement, or at least Scott felt so. The hair on his neck stood straight up – uncertain it was the cold or the presence of someone else. He turned around to see, but there was no one in sight. Again, he felt a whoosh; whatever it was, its movements were fast. Scott closed his eyes to be more in tune with his senses, and to his dismay, his senses were not mistaken. He sensed something moving swiftly through the vacuum of air as if a lion sped toward its prey.

"Who's there?" he cried in urgency.

There was a binding rush of light, a whistling roar in the air, and a ginormous creature seemed to appear out of thin air!!!!

The creature was around 9 feet tall with scaly skin and metallic armor with fluorescent scales. He had abs and muscles. His head and neck were scaly like an alligator and snake combined. With a light green hue to his skin, he had scales on his rubbery skin the color of burnt copper. His face, shaped like a lizard with large eyes, had orange pupils and no irises. His large hands were capped off with metallic gold armor on his fingers that seemed to glow iridescently.

There was no hair on his head; instead, just a Mohawk-shaped bone protruded above his head that also had burnt orange scales. His long limbs with gold-tipped fingers held a torch which he directed at Scott. His face had small holes for nostrils and ears.

Fearful, Scott immediately took a few steps backward, stumbled, and fell to the ground.

'Oh my God, oh my God….who, what are you?' he said, panicking.

11

The creature sized him up from head to toe from afar. It spoke in a blank verse, winding up the effort to utter a few words. Before each sentence, its lips moved silently, and his brows wore an expression of intense concentration.

Scrambling to get to his feet to run away, Scott accidentally hit his chest with his fist, and suddenly, there was a flash, and things went dark.

Thud!! Scott rolled up onto a tree. He sat there, looking a little pained and discombobulated. Rubbing his eyes, trying to adjust his focus on his surroundings after the blinding experience he just went through, AGAIN!!! Not to mention extremely frightening!!!

He stared into the sky, hoping to see some constellation that would help him figure out where he was. Instead, he saw what looked like planets, not just one but three, that seemed to line up perfectly in the distance of space. The first planet was so close that he thought he could touch it. The stars were so bright they seemed to hold hands and dance around the planets in perfect synchrony.

"Well, I'm definitely NOT on Earth!!!" he thought to himself. "What the heck is going on?"

As Scott sat upright, he started to notice his surroundings; he was in what seemed like a forest, except it wasn't like any forest he had ever been to. There were large tree-like shapes, except upside down. The ground near the base was covered in what you would see underwater on a coral reef, and the tree trunk extended into the sky with roots trying to reach even further. The ground danced in brilliant colors of blue, green, red, and orange with similar hues glowing, almost emitting light out of each coral polyp. Scott was in awe as his mind tried to process what his eyes were seeing in disbelief.

Scott finally stood up, still taking in his surroundings. "This is amazing; I can't believe what I'm seeing." He reached over to the upside-down tree, trying to touch the coral-polyp-like stuff on it, but then it suddenly retracted, shrinking into itself almost as though it was hiding, the same way a real coral polyp would. At that very moment, Scott had noticed his hands were not his hands but something different; they were huge, with sharp claw-like nails. His skin was blue with orange lines from the nails running down the middle of each finger and meeting at the middle of his hand, then becoming one and running up his arm. His right shoulder had metallic armor with spikes, and when he looked down, he saw the device he found at the construction site attached to the center of his chest.

Scott yelled, "Oh my God, what is this? What am I? Where did my body go!!!" Scott was really freaked out now and started breathing heavily, panicking; his heart felt like it would jump out of his body.

After a few moments, and a bit calmer, he started to walk through the forest, stumbling here and there. Soon he neared what looked like a lake. Scott was at maximum freak-out mode but steadied himself as he got to his knees and looked into the water; what he saw next almost made him pass out. Looking back at him from the reflection of the water was something he could not fathom. His face was completely different; he had 4 eyes, 2 on each side slightly staggered, his nose looked like three horns with slits on each; the same orange lines that were on his hands came down from the side of his head over his eyes and split over each nostril. His mouth was wide, with somewhat sharp teeth, and his tongue was split in three. Even though his face seemed scary, there was a sense of softness to it, something innocent, as crazy as that sounds, considering how scary Scott looked to himself in this new form.

"I'm a freaking alien!!!" he screamed. He was now living the things that were only in his imagination. He wasn't so scared anymore but more curious about exploring more of the alien planet he was on. He took a couple of sips of water from the alien lake, figuring at this point since he was an alien, it would be harmless, which it turned out to be.

Walking past the water, he noticed some alien creatures running around; they all seemed to remind him of home in a weird way. For instance, there was something that looked like a rabbit that had three tails, huge kangaroo-sized hind legs, t-rex-like arms, and 6 purple eyes. "Hahahaha!" he burst out laughing, taking mental pictures as he continued walking.

He also saw some not-so-funny creepy, crawly serpent-type things, which looked like something out of a sci-fi horror movie. He quickly walked up the hill towards the ridge as fast as he could to get away from the not-so-nice-looking creatures.

At the top of the hill, in the distance, he could see something like a village with huts and camps. It was hard to tell what it was, but at least there was something. He slowly made his way through the now desolate landscape towards the village. As he neared the village, there seemed to be a moat-type feature with pathways at various points. As Scott proceeded to one of the pathways, he looked to the left.

"Oh my God, what is that, are those, are those bones," he exclaimed loudly and, from the shock, lost his balance and fell into the moat. Scott was crying in total panic, and fear took over his entire body. He hastily scrambled through the bones trying to climb out of the moat, grasping at anything he could. Struggling, he grabbed bones in each of his hands and used them like picks to pull himself out of the moat and lay there on the other side, now closer to the village.

Crying and unable to think, "I need to get somewhere to hide; this is not good". He scrambled to his feet, making his way through the dark spots on the path to the village. Hiding and staying out of sight, he found a spot behind a hut-type structure and sat there in the dark, trying to regain his composure. "This is a bad place, this is a very bad place. Who builds a moat with the dead around their village," he thought. "I need to get out of here, somehow." Too scared to leave his spot and be seen, Scott just sat there in silence, hoping the light would not give away his location as he used the darkness for cover. After a few moments, he fell asleep from the exhaustion of everything that had happened so far.

A little while later, Scott was awoken by some rustling sounds around the side of the hut. He carefully looked around the corner and saw what looked like an elderly alien and a smaller one that was about the same size as him. They seemed to be talking, the kid was saying. "Karta, uraga nuu sumoon cal, urga nuu sumoon asa fraat nii ka nova sacray sovaa puruva." Scott was shocked when he actually understood what the kid had said; somehow, it was translated into English. "Dad, I don't want to do this. I don't want to be a prison guard that kills prisoners."

The elderly voice responded, "Atraka, cal nuut sumoon si wa, mir karta cala, iaat friet karmaka so, wa karvasava nova sacray", again Scott could understand, "Child, this is what we do, my father did it, it is what you are supposed to do, we are generations of prison guards."

The child responded, "Yeah, I get that, but why do we have to kill the prisoners." The kid started to walk away towards the back of the hut, shaking his head as his dad stood there with his hands folded across his chest.

Scott quickly and quietly pulled his head back from the edge of the hut and went back to his spot, still in the darkness, and stayed as still as he possibly could. He was scared out of his mind, quivering as he sat there in absolute silence.

Scott watched as the alien kid walked past him, hearing him sob; he felt bad for him. He seemed like any other kid, dealing with the same things most kids deal with their parents. Although every aspect of this situation was different, after all, this was an alien planet, and Scott was more used to disagreements about what was appropriate to wear to church. Nevertheless, Scott still felt empathetic towards the child.

He sat there in silence and prayed, "Please don't turn around, please, please just keep walking away". At that very moment, the alien child turned around and looked at Scott, more bewildered than anything.

"Why are you sitting behind my house in the dark?" the alien child asked quietly and calmly.

Scott stuttered, "Um, I.. I uhhh… I got lost and didn't know where I was. I got scared and hid behind your house and fell asleep. I woke up when I heard you talking. I'm sorry, I did not mean to intrude".

As Scott said this, what he heard was the alien language!!! Somehow, whatever he said was being translated into their language. Scott was perplexed as to how this was possible, and then he looked down at the key on his chest; it was the only logical explanation. It did portal him to this planet and changed his body into a similar form to the alien he saw before him.

The alien child was staring at Scott, "Hello, what happened? You drifted off there for a minute."

"Sorry," replied Scott. "I was just trying to remember how I got lost and then remembered something," quickly trying to divert the topic, he asked, "What's your name?"

"My name is Aegnor," replied the alien child, walking closer to Scott. "What is your name?"

Scott replied, "My name is Scott."

"That's a very unusual name, I don't think I have ever heard that before. Where are you from, Scott?" asked Aegnor.

Scott was getting nervous. He was hoping to end the conversation sooner rather than later, out of fear of what would happen if Aegnor found out he wasn't from this planet.

Scott replied nervously, "I'm from the other side of the planet; it's a small city, quite a ways beyond the forest out there. I'm sure you never heard of it."

Aegnor was a little suspicious because of the vagueness of Scott's answers but did not want to push, sensing he was scared, and he seemed nice after all. "Well, I have done quite a bit of exploring of the planet with my father, but we still have much to see, maybe you can take me to your city one day."

Relieved that the conversation about himself was coming to an end, Scott replied, "Yeah, one day!!!" Scott slowly stood up from his hiding spot, trying to think of a way to get out of his current situation, even though he didn't feel like he was in danger. He didn't think it was wise to continue to engage the locals, but he also had no idea what to do next; after all, he was on an alien planet!!!

"You're pretty dirty and banged up. Do you want to come over, get cleaned up, and maybe have some food? I'm sure my parents won't mind," asked Aegnor

Scott didn't know what to do, he didn't know where to go. He thought to himself, "I have two choices, stay here, get cleaned up and have some food, maybe even a bed to sleep in, or touch this thing on my chest and run into a 9-foot alien that would eat me!!!!" The choice seemed pretty clear.

All things considered, it was a quick and easy decision to make, after all. Scott replied, "Thank you, Aegnor, I would love to get cleaned up and have some food."

Aegnor and Scott made their way from behind the hut towards the front. As they approached the front door of Aegnor's house, they noticed some increased activity in the vicinity but didn't pay much attention to it as they entered the house.

As they walked into the house, Scott was blown away by how technologically advanced the house looked inside—considering it looked like a simple hut from the outside. In the room, directly in front of the door they had just entered, was a large room with what looked like 3 TVs floating in the air, but it was just that – a screen floating in the air. It looked like you could literally put your hand through it. It was almost like a holographic image, but Scott had no idea where they were coming from. Even the seats around the screens seemed to float in the air and were made of some sort of energy. Scott's mind was whirling; he was a techy after all.

To the left of that room was what looked like a kitchen, but it was like no kitchen he had ever seen. There seemed to be robot hands coming out of the wall at each end of what looked like a stove area, and the thing that looked like a fridge seemed to be made of glass or something. It was completely transparent, and upon looking closer, he wondered if there was even glass there. He was hearing a humming sound. There was, maybe, some sort of a forcefield around the food in the fridge?

"Dad, I met someone when I was out walking after our talk. He isn't from here and seems to have gotten lost. I wanted to help him out. Would it be ok if he gets cleaned up and has dinner with us?" Aegnor asked.

Aegnor's dad, Stregnor, was sitting in the hall, deep in thought over the conversation with Aegnor earlier. "Sure, son, your friend can stay. What's his name?" asked Stregnor.

"His name is Scott," replied Aegnor.

Stregnor looked up, seeing Scott next to his son. "Well, that's an unusual name. Nice to meet you, Scott. Welcome to our house."

"Thank you, Mr. Stregnor. I really appreciate your kindness," said Scott as he and Aegnor made their way down the hall.

"Hold on, Scott, what is Mister? Why did you call me Mister Stregnor? What does that mean?"

Scott stopped dead in his tracks, stunned, shocked, and turned around slowly, trying to think of what to say. "Ummm, ahhh well... Where I'm from... I mean, I once traveled to this planet with my parents. On that planet, kids used that word as a sign of respect to elders, so I kinda liked it, and whenever I meet a friend's parents or something, I call them by Mister or Misses and their last name."

"Last name? What's that?" asked Stregnor.

Again Scott stuttered, "Um, well, um, they have like 2 names, the last name is like their house name. So either all the family members will have the dad's or mom's as a last name; it's how they identify they belong to the family."

"Hmmmm, that's very interesting, Scott. In our culture, our first names are the designation for us – we are the *egnors, so anyone in our family will have names that end with that. Similarly, there are others like the *ratnus, *cravars, etc..." that live in this compound," said Stregnor. "We can chat more once you have cleaned yourself up."

Scott took a deep breath and turned back around to see Aegnor looking at him oddly. Like, what the hell is this kid talking about? Scott knew all this must be really weird for them to hear; it was weird for him, considering what he had to explain. Scott was not looking forward to any more talks, but that seemed inevitable. He would have to think of more alien-like stuff to say."

Both kids finally made it to Aegnor's room, which also seemed to be fashioned in the same way the living room was, except for large floating screens. The screens actually seemed to be the entire wall, and a bed that appeared to be made out of energy floated in the air. The only thing that looked like a solid object was the desk and walls. Scott noticed the desk was very similar to his, ordained with what looked like tools and parts of things that he imagined Aegnor must have taken apart.

"Scott, you can go into the bathroom just past the screens and get cleaned up," Aegnor instructed.

"Umm, what do you mean just past the screens? There's nothing there, just a wall," Scott said, very confused.

Aegnor replied cockily, "You really aren't from around here, these walls are photonic illusions you can just walk through, I can't see you, and you can't see me."

Scott was in awe hearing about such things – this was his dream come true. The technology he had only ever seen in the movies was right here, at his fingertips. He made his way into the bathroom through the screens that were also photonic walls. "Wow, this is so cool," he thought to himself as he now stood in a square room.

As if things weren't weird enough, he stood there looking around for a tub, shower, and faucet, but nothing was there. He thought for a minute as he took off the armor from his right shoulder and the belt underwear thing that he had on but now, thinking about it, he didn't even know it was on him till just now. As he undressed, a portion of the wall seemed to depress almost into a closet. He assumed he was supposed to put his armor and belt underwear thing in there, and he did. To his surprise, they stayed there in mid-air, floating in exactly the place he put them. Then suddenly, he heard a hissing, almost misting sound, and then there was a laser light sheet that came from the top of the closet over his armor and belt underwear. It was fascinating. The next thing he knew, his armor shined brightly, and his underwear belt was a few shades lighter.

As he turned away from the closet and thought about how he was going to get cleaned, he heard the same hissing, almost misting sound. "What the heck, where is that coming from," he thought. Then he started to see something wet on his body; he could feel it too. Then he saw the same laser light sheet, except they were coming at him from all directions like the whole room was closing in on him. "This is so cool," he thought, and within seconds, the room was back to its shape. He was dry and assumed clean and proceeded to put on his underwear belt and held onto his armor as he felt he didn't need to wear it for the night.

Scott walked back into the room through the walls. He still couldn't get over the whole experience. "That was the coolest shower I have ever had," he exclaimed to Aegnor.

Aegnor looked at Scott, perplexed. "What is a shower?"

Scott thought to himself, "Oh man, I did it again, I'm totally gonna blow it if I keep this up. I gotta stop using words they don't understand, but how the heck am I going to do that."

"Oh, that just means getting cleaned up. It's one of those things I picked up when I traveled with my parents," Scott replied, hoping that would end it.

Aegnor looked at Scott like he was the weirdest alien he had ever met. "Well, let's go and eat, I'm starving."

Aegnor and Scott made their way to the living room through the hall, which, this time, Scott noticed had digital pictures of what looked like a family that seemed to appear and disappear along the wall as they walked by. He was again in awe of the technology that enabled this.

"Welcome back, boys, are you ready to eat?" asked Stregnor as the boys approached.

Aegnor and Scott replied at the same time as they sat down at the table, "We sure are!!!"

Stregnor brought the food from the kitchen and placed it on the table in front of each of the kids and then himself. "Well, Scott, I hope you're hungry. I made some fresh fraklack and strastick."

Scott looked at the plate in front of him and did not know what he was looking at. It had what looked like slimy snakes that kinda looked like noodles, which were green, with round orange-colored balls, like meatballs, and something else that seemed to move in and out of the food, "God, I hope this tastes like chicken," he thought.

Scott kindly said, "This looks amazing, it smells delicious," and very cautiously took a small bite of the fraklack. "Wow!!!! This really is delicious Mr.Stregnor."

Scott was now eating heaping spoons at a time, famished from everything that had happened since the construction site.

Realizing he was eating so quickly without even looking up, Scott slowed down. "I'm so sorry, I haven't had anything to eat since I got lost."

"It's ok," Stregnor replied. "We understand. Eat as much as you want. If you like, you can stay the night too. It wouldn't be wise for you to try and find your way home at night. Also, it's not often we get visitors, and there are not many kids here, so I think Aegnor would love to have you as well."

Aegnor replied excitedly, "Really, dad, thanks. Can Scott and I go outside after dinner?"

"Are you sure? I really don't want to impose," said Scott politely, but he really felt much better knowing he wouldn't have to go out on his own tonight and had a safe place to stay."

"I don't see why not, but stay inside the perimeter of the compound, and only for a little while, it's almost time for bed," said Stregnor.

Scott and Aegnor quickly finished their meals, excited to go out and hang out!!! Scott brought his plate to the kitchen area, not entirely sure where to put it. He placed it on the countertop where he thought the sink should be, which is usually across from the stove, which, well, he didn't exactly know where that was either, but assumed it was somewhere between the robot hands.

As he placed it down, the countertop seemed to disappear from underneath, and the plate slowly lowered into the newly revealed basin and just floated there. Next, the same laser light sheet that his armor and himself got cleaned in came out from all sides of the basin, and just like that, the plate was clean and then seconds later disappeared into the wall of the basin. Scott stood there, again, in awe of what he was seeing. He felt it was better to keep his awe to himself than express or say anything out loud, trying to avoid any more questions that may give away the fact that he was not alien or from this planet.

Aegnor called out to Scott, "Hey, are you ready to go out? There are some really cool things in the compound."

Scott asked, slightly confused, "There are? When I saw this place, it looked like a small village."

"Oh, well, that's what it looks like from above, but there's a whole underground part," Aegnor replied

"Dad, is it ok if I show him?" asked Aegnor.

"Sure, take this visitor's pass and remember to stay away from the restricted areas," Stregnor replied as he reached into his pack and grabbed the pass for the kids.

Aegnor grabbed the pass from his dad, and he and Scott headed out the front door.

Scott was excited to explore with Aegnor. He thought to himself, "An underground part, I wonder what that could be."

As they walked out into the compound, passing more hut-like structures, Scott noticed the perfectly symmetrical setup of all the huts. From Aegnor's house, they passed at least 3 sets or rows of huts, and as they neared the center, he looked around; the huts were all in a circle. He couldn't help but ask, "So Aegnor, what is the underground place?"

Aegnor replied as he started to pull the pass out of his pack, "Well, you will see," and he waved the pass in the air. Then as if out of thin air, a half-circle dome appeared.

Scott was astonished at what he saw; the dome seemed to have the same photonic walls he saw in Aegnor's room. "Whoaaa," he exclaimed.

"Come on, follow me. Just have to walk through," Aegnor said as he proceeded through the photonic wall into the dome.

Scott followed without question and soon stood inside the dome. It was bright inside, with white blueish tones moving like waves through the white. He could hear a slight humming sound. He assumed that it was from whatever energy was creating the dome. As he stood there next to Aegnor, the dome started to descend into the ground. Slowly both their bodies started to disappear into the solid ground they were standing on. Scott stood there watching as his knees started to vanish below him, but he was calm. This was just the next weird thing to happen to him; it was starting to feel normal to be in unbelievable situations. As the ground neared his head, he took a deep breath and closed his eyes as if he was going underwater, he didn't know why he did that, but he did.

Scott exhaled, opened his eyes, and what he saw blew his mind away. He now stood in what looked like a city. It was bright, with aliens of all sorts bustling around.

There were shops and what looked like restaurants, or at least he assumed when he saw a sign for fresh fraklak and strastick posted on the window. Scott still didn't know what part of the meal he ate was fraklak if that was the noodles, and what part was strastick, if that was the weird thing crawling in and out of his food or the things that looked like meatballs.

"Wow, Aegnor, how big is this place?" Scott asked since the street didn't seem to end as far as he could see.

"Well, this level runs for miles in every direction. This street we are on is where we come to shop, eat and relax. There are three more levels beneath us. Let's walk around a bit, and I'll take you down."

They both started walking down the street. Scott, of course, was trying to take in everything he was seeing. The street was brightly lit, but it wasn't all from lights; there was a sky, but that didn't make sense since they were underground. Scott figured it must be some sort of holograph built into this place to simulate daytime.

They walked past a shop that looked like it sold weapons. On display, he saw something that looked like an axe, except at the bottom part of the handle, there was a blade that was almost transparent. He figured it was some sort of laser blade or something. Then along the handle near the bottom and about midway up, there were spikes, and the axe part itself was also kinda transparent like the blade. Again, Scott thought it must be some sort of laser blade that he was sure could slice through just about anything.

As Scott was looking at the different places, Aegnor grabbed his hand and took him inside one of the establishments. Scott didn't see what from the outside, but once inside, he looked around and saw aliens flying in the air above him. It sounded like a lights-saber "Kwishuuuuuuuuuu" in bursts, pops of bright-colored streaks from one alien to another, then one of them emitting a bright green flash.

"Whoaa, how are they… what are they doing up there?" asked Scott.

Aegnor replied, "Ohh, that's a game called "Scritsvat". Each player has on a "skynak" suit which allows them to essentially fly around, and they each have a gun that shoots photonic bullets. No player dies till all the players have shot them, or the player shoots all the other players. The player with the most kills at the end of the round wins. The guns are set to low power, so the bullets just hit you and push you back and trigger the points counter for your color. There are lots of good places to hide out and take long-range shots without ever being seen, ah, and umm... having a couple of shooter upgrades. I have one of the highest records here!!!"

"That looks like so much fun!!!" Scott exclaimed as he laughed, sheer joy emanating from him.

This was the first time he felt like he had a friend, you know... before kids grew up and were mean for no reason. He was still Scott, even though he didn't look like Scott, he was still Scott, and Aegnor totally dug hanging out with him.

Everything that happened till now felt like a thing of the past; he was feeling amazing!!!

Aegnor again grabbed Scott's hand and swung him around to face a black circle that seemed to swirl.

Shocked, Scott jumped back three spaces, almost knocking over Aegnor.

"Whoaaa, you ok... I'm so sorry, Scott, I didn't mean to scare you. I saw how amazed you were when you saw "Scritsvat". I was excited to show you this!!! This is called "troas"."

Scott was steadying himself as he looked at this big floating black circle that swirled. Now a few feet back, he noticed the outer part of the circle had a white glowing light around it as if holding it in. Above that was the end of what was shaped like a horseshoe or those U-shaped magnets, and this thin as paper black hole just floated there.

He didn't feel so amazed at the moment; he was feeling a little jittery.

"Scott, it's ok, just relax, we are going in together. Let me ask you something, what would be the coolest thing you would want to do if you could?" asked Aegnor, noticing Scott shaking a little.

Feeling better, they would go in together. Scott jokingly replied, "I don't know, ride an asteroid."

"Ok, done. Stand right here. I'll be right back, I promise," said Aegnor as he approached the black circle.

Scott watched as Aegnor took out his pass, waved it in the air, and a screen appeared out of nowhere, just floating there in front of Aegnor on which he saw him type a bunch of things.

"Ummm, what's going on?" asked Scott as Aegnor made his way back.

"Don't worry, trust me," replied Aegnor, now standing beside Scott in front of the black circle that swirled. He took Scott's hand and jumped into the circle, pulling Scott in beside him.

"It's ok, you can open your eyes, Scott," said Aegnor calmly.

"My eyes are open. They were open the whole time!!!!!" said Scott excitedly.

"Hahaaahaaaa, well, why aren't they open then!!!!" Aegnor laughed.

Scott burst out laughing as well and opened his eyes. "Oh my gosh, where are we?"

He stared out over the rough and jagged surface to see the open space in front of him with flashing streaks of yellow and red zipping all around him. He turned to his left to see what looked like three planets with the stars almost stacked on top of each other, and below that, he assumed, was the planet he was on.

He turned to see Aegnor smiling at him. "You said you wanted to ride an asteroid, so here you are, you're riding an asteroid!!!"

"Are you kidding me? How is this even possible!" Scott asked

"Well, the aliens that own "Scritsvat" came up with this crazy idea a few years ago to put a receiver on the asteroid that circles our planet and have a portal that would let you, well, ride an asteroid," replied Aegnor.

After a few moments, Aegnor called to Scott, "You ready to go? We have to get home soon, we can be a little late, but not too late, or my dad will have me working night shifts at the prison, and I really don't like that. I still want to show you the other levels before we go."

"No, I mean yeah, haha, how could you ever want to leave this? It's just so cool," Scott said and went to grab Aegnor's hand to jump back through the black circle.

As they appeared on the other side, back at "Scritsvat" laughing, they were greeted by two dozen guards.

Taking a step forward and almost falling backward, they both exclaimed, "What's going on?!" in complete shock at being surrounded by prison guards.

"You come with us," said the large prison guard looking at Scott with half his face covered in a red-metallic helmet.

"Wait, what? Why? I didn't do anything," Scott said, with fear in his voice.

The large prison guard quickly approached Scott and grabbed both his hands by the wrist, lifting him into the air and placing cuffs on him.

Aegnor yelled, "Wait, stop, listen to me, please. My father is Stregnor, he works here. This is Scott, my friend. Please just let him go, and we can call my dad, and he will sort this all out."

The other guards quickly formed a circle around the large prison guard, pushing Aegnor to the side. They all proceeded to march in unison out of "Scritsvat".

Aegnor watched as his friend was being taken away. He knew Scott was good; he sensed it. Even though they only knew each other for so long, he felt Scott was a friend, a good friend. Gathering himself together, Aegnor started to run out of "Scritsvat" towards his home.

As Scott hung there in the large guard's hands, bound by cuffs that looked to be made of energy, he cried out, "Please, please let me go. I didn't do anything wrong!!!

The guards ignored him as they walked with their heads up and continued down the street, passing all the shops. They turned a corner around a building that didn't have any windows and now stood in front of it.

Scott watched helplessly as the guard from the back made his way to the front and waved his hand in a Z pattern, then up from the bottom point of the Z in a straight line to the top point of the Z, then circled around the top to the right to the bottom point of the Z.

Just like that, the walls of the building began to open, revealing what looked like an office. Scott thought to himself, this must be like a police station or something. He looked around, still in tears and scared about what was going to happen.

As they made their way in, towards what looked like gates standing in front of a large rectangular box made of light, Scott looked around hopelessly, then suddenly felt a cold shudder go through his body when he saw an alien pointing at him, talking to another alien behind the glass. It was the same alien he saw when he first got to the planet and was in the dry arid place. Scott felt more hopeless than ever. He was trying to figure out what was going on.

As his mind whirled, almost making him dizzy, he watched blankly as the alien that was pointing at him now stood in front of him. The alien stared at him, dead in the eyes. "Not getting away this time," he growled in a deep raspy voice.

Scott felt his heart drop to the bottom of his stomach. He thought to himself, "They must think I'm a prisoner and that I escaped or something. This isn't happening. What am I going to do!!!"

The guards lifted Scott back up and proceeded through the gates into the large rectangular box.

Again the guard in the back turned to face the wall of the box they were in and waved his hand in the same pattern as before, and the box started to descend through the floor.

Scott watched as they continued down through what seemed like a few floors. He thought, "If only I had some weapons, something, anything to get free, I could make a run for it." Just as the thought entered his mind, blades of light came out of his arms, from his elbows to his wrist, cutting the cuffs and setting him free, dropping him to the floor. He kneeled there for a second as the walls of the rectangular light box slowly opened to reveal what looked like a labyrinth of rooms with white glowing fields in front of each room. He could barely make out something moving in a few of them.

Scott jumped into a sprint running straight ahead, not knowing what else to do. He wasn't a fighter; he couldn't fight the guards. He didn't know what was now on his arms or what they could do, even though he saw them cut through the cuffs.

The guards chased Scott down the pathway. Scott thought to himself as he cried, running, "This is it, it's a prison, I'm done. I'm never going to get out of here. I'll never see Zero or my parents!!!"

Scott felt helpless as he neared what looked like a dead-end. He turned and dropped one knee to the floor. He kneeled there, thinking it was the end. He felt like he was being bullied, but this was the worst version of it ever. He started to get angry. He was so happy he met Aegnor. He had felt happiness for the first time in a long time; he had made a friend… and that was all being taken away. He screamed out loud in rage as he stood up and felt a surge of power building up in his chest. Then suddenly, a burst of light came out from him, knocking over all the guards around and sending him hurling backward, rolling over and over again till he hit a wall.

Scott slowly sat up, feet laid out in front of him, feeling discombobulated from what just happened. He stared at a wall, his vision a little blurred. "What was that?!!!" he said, shaking his head left to right.

As his vision started to clear, he started to get to his feet. Still staring at the wall, he slowly turned his head only to see the same white glowing field he saw in the rooms when the door of the rectangular box opened; it now stood in front of him.

He banged on it with his fist, and his arm was blown back as if the light wall punched him back. "Whaaaaaaattttttttttt! Oh no, what!!! I'm in a cell!!!!" Panicking, he hit his chest repeatedly, but nothing was happening; Scott fell down to his knees, sobbing.

Just then, the ceiling in front of the field that kept him in the cell came crashing down.

Scott looked up with tears in his eyes and could barely make out a figure behind the cloud of dust; rubbing his eyes, he watched as it approached.

3.

Quastaro Noor

"I can help you, just grab my hand and think of the last place you felt safe, then hit your chest," said the voice, almost angelic sounding.

"I can't. I just tried hitting my chest over and over again, and nothing happened, and I can't grab your hand. This light wall forces me back when I touch it," Scott said, frustrated.

"Grab my hand when I put it through and hit your chest, and don't forget to think of the place you last felt safe," said the alien again.

Scott was confused; how was it possible that she could pass through this light wall, he thought. He then reached up to grab the hand that was now inside the cell.

He did as he was told and hit his chest. "Whooooooosh," a bright light engulfed them, and they both now stood in Aegnor's bedroom.

Aegnor jumped back in shock, almost knocking over his things on the shelf. "What the!!!! Where, how...how did, what!!! How are you here?" he asked, completely bewildered that his friend now stood in front of him.

"Who are you," Aegnor quickly asked as he noticed a female alien holding Scott's hand.

Scott had a feeling it was an alien girl but had just really noticed it since everything that happened was sending adrenaline rushing through his body. He quickly pulled his hand away, suddenly feeling shy.

The alien girl responded, "My name is Skyla, I was trying to escape the prison when I saw your friend burst into light and knock all the prison guards out. Then I saw him get knocked into the prison cell and get stuck. I couldn't just leave him there. What are your names?"

"My name is Scott, and this is my friend Aegnor. Thank you for saving me!!! I thought my life was over," Scott said, staring at Skyla.

She was about 4'9" and had a slender figure. Her eyes were a crystaline blue, and her skin seemed to be a pearly white color, with hues of blue that seemed random at first but, looking closer, were part of something larger. Her hair was almost white, with blue streaks, and was braided tightly on both sides. Then there were what looked like tentacles above that, and in the center, her hair flowed freely, mostly covering everything else. It was long, almost down below her waist. She wore what looked like a skin-tight suit with a belt hanging on her waist, ordained with various pouches and devices.

Scott was speechless as he found her to be quite beautiful.

"We need to get out of here, every guard on this planet will be looking for you, and probably me as well," Skyla started.

Just then, Stregnor's voice called through the door, "Aegnor, who are you talking to?"

Aegnor was about to reply when his door opened abruptly. All three of the kids stood there frozen.

Stregnor stood there in shock. "Scott!!! How did you get here? Aegnor came running home and told me that guards had taken you prisoner at Scritsvat's. What happened? Why did they take you in?"

"I don't know, I didn't do anything, I swear Mr. Stregnor, when I got here I was lost and saw what I now know was a guard, he stood over me, and I was scared, and I panicked and, and tried to run. The next thing I knew, I was in the forest behind your hut," Scott replied

Scott didn't want to tell him about the device or how it did what it did. He was scared.

"We need to go," said Skyla looking at Aegnor and Scott.

"Who are you!!!" Stregnor interrupted.

"I'm Skyla. I was taken from my home planet for no reason," she responded.

Stregnor knew how this prison and its guards worked. He knew that innocent people were taken from all over the galaxy, held, and even killed here all the time. He worked and lived here because he had no choice, it was all he had ever known, and he had a child to raise. He also knew they would be knocking on his door any minute since Aegnor was with Scott at Scritsvat. He knew what he had to do.

He ran out the door, down the hall towards his room, returning moments later with three solid boxes in his hands.

"Here, take these, one for each of you. You need to get out of here before the guards come through our front door."

"Why three, dad?" asked Aegnor

"You can't stay here anymore, son, the guards saw you with Scott, you have to go with them," Stregnor replied, tears in his eyes.

Aegnor's heart dropped; his whole world just came crashing down. He started to cry. "But dad, I don't want to?"

Stregnor walked to Aegnor and hugged him as hard as he could. "You have to, son!!! This isn't a choice. We will find a way to back to each other again, but till then, you have to go!!!"

Scott and Skyla watched, both with tears in their eyes; they knew how it felt to be away from family, and they understood the deep sadness that it caused.

Skyla and Scott reached for their boxes, which had straps on them so they could wear them over their shoulders. As they put the straps over their head onto their shoulders, they both walked up to Aegnor. "You're with us now, and we promise you will see your dad again!!!!"

Aegnor looked at the both of them with tears in his eyes and grabbed his box and put the strap over his head onto his shoulders, and looked at his dad. "I love you."

Skyla took Scott's hand in hers and instructed Aegnor to take the other in his.

"Scott, you need to say or think "Quastaro Noor" and hit your chest. This will take us to my home planet," Skyla instructed.

Wondering for a moment how Skyla knew what he had to do, Scott said "Quastaro Noor" out loud, and then Whooooosh, a bright light flashed, and they were gone. Stregnor stood there, alone, wide-eyed, his cheeks still wet from the tears of having to say goodbye to his son.

Just then, there was banging at Stregnor's door. As he made his way down the hall to open the door, there stood half a dozen guards.

Scott, Aegnor, and Skyla landed on the ground with a thud, still holding hands.

Scott looked around at his surroundings; they were much different than the last planet he was on. He stood at the top of a hill overlooking a beautiful and what looked like a modern city that was surrounded by lush lawns and a brilliantly colorful forest. He could see creatures flying in the air, he couldn't quite make them out, but they looked graceful as they moved along the sky, which was painted in bright and dark blue, streaks of white and orange flowing through it. He could see shooting stars that looked like they were surfing the different colored streaks. Beyond that was what he thought might be a planet, but it seemed to glow a blueish color that lit the ground below. He thought maybe it was a Moon or something. It was huge, like really huge; he felt tiny looking at it.

35

"Scott, Aegnor, welcome to my home. Scott, thank you for saving me and getting me off that planet," Skyla said joyfully and sincerely as she looked deep into his eyes.

"Those eyes are the most beautiful I have ever seen. She is the most beautiful girl I have ever seen," Scott thought to himself.

"I didn't do anything. If it wasn't for you, Skyla, I would still be stuck in that prison," said Scott humbly.

Aegnor was still sad over leaving his father but still managed to look around. He turned to look at Scott and fell backward. "Who are you? Where's Scott?" he yelled.

"Wait, what, what do you mean? I'm right here, Aegnor," said Scott.

"I hear you, Scott, and see that the voice is coming from the body in front of me, but you're, not you," Aegnor exclaimed

Skyla burst out laughing, "Baahhaaaaahahaaa."

Scott was confused, then looked at his hands. "Ahhhhh, what the heck, what...what am I," he yelled, even though he knew the device did something to him; it was still new to him.

Skyla again burst out laughing hysterically, falling to the ground "Hahahaa, you, you're a quastarian, you look like my people."

Scott looked down at the rest of his body, he was wearing something that was tight on his skin, covering him from his waist down to his knees, and the top was tight as well, with no sleeves, around his waist a belt like Skyla's with pouches, tools and what may be a weapon. He now had the same pearly white skin but dark hues of blue that were more prominent than Skyla's. He had well-kept nails and felt around his body, and he had a pretty fit physique. He ran his hands over his head, it was smooth on both sides, and on top, there was long jet black hair that went to his shoulders. On the back of his head, he could feel something protruding; it was round and seemed to be long. He grabbed it and brought it in front of him so he could see. To his surprise, it was a tentacle, like the ones Skyla had on each side of her head. He felt he looked pretty cool.

Scott looked at Skyla as she lay there on the floor, still giggling. "How are you ok with this and laughing? You saw me looking like one alien, then another, and you laughed. You knew exactly what I needed to do to portal out of prison to Aegnor's house, and you knew what I needed to do to get here. Why is none of this shocking to you the way it is to Aegnor and me?" asked Scott.

Skyla casually sat up, holding her knees in her hands. "Well, it's because you have the Agatova Device," she said in a matter-of-fact tone.

"The what," exclaimed Scott and Aegnor at the same time.

"Well, it's a long story, one that my parents told me, and their parents told them, and so on. Too long a story to tell now, but basically, the Agatovians were a highly advanced alien species that created the device in an effort to go around the universe to teach, enable, educate, provide resources and grow each planet to advance them. It is said they intended to bring peace to the universe to better protect, preserve and evolve the future of all life forms. The device itself has the technology to do… well, what it did to you. It could portal you to any planet you could think of. It would know the planet and the species and give the holder of the device the ability to understand and speak the language, the body, clothes, and tools they need to blend in. They were known for blending in. They felt that the less the species on the planet knew about them, the better. It allowed for a more natural growth. So, they would arrive looking like us, making discoveries, inventing, and creating new things, then just give it to society and disappear."

Aegnor stared in silence at Scott, still trying to fix the image in his head of his friend looking like him, then looking like a boy version of Skyla.

Scott's mind was whirling as he sat on the ground next to Skyla.

"There are stories about the device, like fairytales. That one day, it would be found, and that person would be the key to freeing everyone. Only that person could unlock the power!!!" Skyla said softly as she turned her head to look at Scott.

Scott looked back at her questioningly. "Wait, so, so... you're saying I'm that person?"

"Well, aren't you? You have the device, you changed your original form to the alien on the last planet, then to the alien that stands before me, and most important of all, you're able to activate the power of the device. I was trying to escape and was in the ceiling of the prison when I saw you running out of the rectangular box with blades along your arms. Then there was a burst of light that came out of you and knocked all the guards out. According to the stories, only the person that is meant to have the device can do that. It was then that I knew I had to help you."

Scott stared out into the sky. "Why me? I'm just a kid who gets bullied and pushed around. I've never stood up for myself. I spend most of my time alone. The only thing I'm good at is video games and building stuff from nothing."

Skyla inched closer and put her arm around him over his shoulders. "It's said the device doesn't pick a person based on WHAT they are, but WHO they are inside and what they can be; there's a reason for all of this that no one knows except for the Agatovians. As far as I can tell, you are the one!!!"

Hearing Aegnor make his way over, Scott turned his head and laughed, "Haha! Finally, on your feet."

"Oh man, this is the craziest thing I've ever been through!!! Scott, I can't believe this, this is amazing, and don't worry, you have me by your side!!!" said Aegnor, now standing next to Skyla and Scott.

"And me, of course!!!" said Skyla excitedly. "Now come, you two, let's try to cover as much ground as we can before nightfall."

All three of them stared one last time out into the horizon over the beautiful city in the distance and started to make their way down the hill.

The hill had a gradual descent, a bit of dirt at the top just before the descent started, then filling in with foliage as it neared the bottom. The ground was covered in purple squares sticking out of the ground with what looked like leaves hugging it from all sides. It seemed to be the most dominant plant as far as he could see, then in random pops were these flat cone-like, orange, circular-shaped bunches that looked like they were headbanging to their favorite song as they danced in the wind.

Scott seemed ok on the outside, holding it together as he walked, but inside, he was scared and overwhelmed, but at the same time felt happy and safe with his new friends besides him. He felt with Skyla and Aegnor by his side, he could do anything.

As they neared the bottom of this hill, they came to what looked like a river of crystals; it was beautiful as it reflected the colors of the evening sky. The river wasn't too deep; they wouldn't be more than waist deep if they walked across.

"This is the river "Kirti", she flows from high up in the mountains far away from here, it is said the crystals are made naturally from the minerals in the mountain and along the way. This is one of the parts of the river with the highest concentration of crystals. It has healing and energy properties. When we walk in, we will feel reenergized, and any wounds that are not too serious will be healed." said Skyla.

39

Scott was so fascinated by this he immediately stepped into the water. It felt freezing at first, till he realized it was just a tingly sensation that felt cold, but it really wasn't. He could feel something in his feet whirling up inch by inch as each part of his body entered the water. It felt rejuvenating, invigorating, and energetic.

Now all three of them were waist deep in the river, holding hands as they made their way to the other side.

Scott could feel something brushing up against his legs as he walked and was a little shocked at first till he looked down and saw a bunch of brilliantly colored creatures playing in the water by his feet, legs, and around his waist. They were like fish, but they looked like they had fur which moved in waves with their bodies in the water. They were all different colors with bright yellow eyes and seemed friendly.

"What are these creatures?" asked Scott.

Looking down to see what he was talking about, Skyla replied, "Oh, those things are "shuktriis", they live on the land and In the water. They maintain the balance of life in the river, all the way from the mountain tops. They are the dominant species in the river. Friendly, until they are balancing life, then they can be a bit vicious. It is their job, after all." replied Skyla laughingly.

They were all now almost out of the water, making their way to the flat land at the riverbank.

Just then, Scott shrieked, looking at Skyla, "I'm glowing, why am I glowing? Wait, why are you glowing? What is going on?"

Skyla burst out laughing. "I told you…the river has healing and energy properties, and for us specifically, it revitalizes the cells in our bodies, causing us to glow, the glow only lasts for a little while, but the extra energy you feel will last for days."

40

"Whoa, I thought I felt it before in the water, but now yeah, I can feel it even more. I feel stronger, more alert, like everything in me is supercharged," Scott exclaimed with a smile on his face as he looked at Skyla.

Still glowing, except for Aegnor, they proceed to walk. Just a few feet ahead, there was a forest that glowed in brilliant colors that were beyond even that of a rainbow Scott observed.

"That is the "Forest of Fraknulan"; it is home to most of the creatures that live here," said Skyla as they neared the edge of the forest.

Scott and Aegnor stood there in awe of the beauty in front of them.

"Why are the trees glowing like that? What are those bright lights running like veins, Skyla?" asked Aegnor as he approached the trunk of one of the trees. Reaching out to touch it out of curiosity.

"Nooooo!!!!!!! Don't touch it, or else you'll burn up from the inside and explode," yelled Skyla.

Aegnor stopped dead in his tracks and stumbled backward, almost falling "Ahhhhh! Oh my God! Why didn't you tell me sooner? I could have died!!!" he yelled.

"Baahaahahaa," Skyla laughed, unable to contain herself for scaring Aegnor.

Aegnor looked at her, eyes squinting, "Not funny, Skyla, not funny at all," with a smirk on his face.

"Hahaha, I'm sorry, Aegnor, you can touch the tree. I couldn't resist, it was perfect. Wish you could have seen your face," she laughed.

Scott watched as the two were getting along. It made him happy that they felt close enough to have fun at each other's expense. This was his family now. He felt it in his bones.

"The tree absorbs the groundwater from the river. The same thing that happens to Scott and me is what's happening to the tree. It is with this energy it can grow and provide for the creatures of the forest. Everything on this planet is connected in one way or another," said Skyla.

Scott and Aegnor listened as they both stood at their own tree with their hands on it.

"I can feel it, I can feel it pulsating through me, then back out through my hand into the tree; this is amazing," said Aegnor, finally feeling what Scott and Skyla had felt when they were in the water.

He didn't have the same feeling they had in the water, his feeling was different, but he didn't want to say anything. He figured it had something to do with Skyla's species because of what she said earlier about how it specifically revitalizes their cells, causing them to glow. Also, they were the only two glowing!!!

Scott supportively said, "Yeah, this is amazing. I feel... I feel like... like I'm connected to everything. Wow."

Skyla called out, "Okay, come on, guys. I want to get to a certain point in the forest before we stop for the night."

Aegnor and Scott pulled their hands away from the trees and started to follow Skyla into the brightly illuminated forest. Both still feeling the effects of the tree.

As they walked, Scott was looking at everything. Absorbing the beauty around him.

He saw a koala-like creature, but even cuter, clinging to the trunk of a tree. It had blue hair, with a white mohawk from its head to its tail, its ears flopped over both eyebrows, and big gray puppy-dog eyes as it watched them walk by.

Then all of a sudden, out of nowhere, Scott is thrown forward into Skyla, knocking her forward onto her knees, almost onto her face, had she not thrown her hands in front of her at the last moment.

"Ahhhhh, what the -_ what is this?! I can feel it, get it off me! What is this?!" Scott screamed as he felt something moving around his body very quickly. "Help guys, help, please get it off me!"

Aegnor was helping Skyla up, and they both turned in a panic. Then they both stared with a smirk on their face.

"Why are you smirking at…, what's going on…, what's on me?!" he yelled, just as he saw a tail whip by his face.

Facing Scott now, Skyla yelled, "Relax, Scott. It's a "Grabtrilop" friendly and very playful. It doesn't mean you any harm. Put your arms out and touch finger tip to finger tip, close each side finger by finger till only the finger that touched the whole time is left, and hold."

Calm now, hearing from Skyla, Scott did as instructed, and within seconds, he saw a red-haired, white-pawed, 4-legged, 4-armed, 4-eyed monkey with ears just big enough to see through hair and a tail ten times his size, dangling on his two touching fingers.

"What the…? When that thing crawled off my shoulders, it was like 4 feet long, and now it's less than a foot, dangling between my fingers. This is the coolest animal ever!!!" Scott yelled.

And just like that, the Grabtrilop was gone. All they could hear were the sounds of the forest

"We gotta go guys, no more "sight-seeing"!!!" yelled Skyla.

Scott and Aegnor came up behind Skyla quickly as she continued down a path she knew all too well.

"You know, I wouldn't exactly call that near-death experience sight-seeing," Scott yelled jokingly, knowing the response he would get back.

43

As expected, they both stopped dead in their tracks, turned with what they thought was a stern face, when really it looked like a stern face ready to explode, and then "Bahahahaaaaaa!" they exploded into laughter; Scott did the same.

Quickly helping Aegnor and Scott get to their feet, Skyla says, "We are almost there."

Moving so quickly through the forest, there were far fewer chances for distraction, and in a short time, they were in a not-so-wooded part of the forest.

"Phweeeehh," said Scott breathlessly as he listened to Aegnor behind him, taking gasps of air.

As Skyla walked closer to Scott, she quickly turned her head and pointed her hand behind her, back to the empty plot of land. "We are here."

"We are where? I don't see anything," Aegnor said bluntly as he got to his feet.

At the same time, Scott was getting to his feet, looking at Agenor with a confused look, and they both stood there and stared as Skyla walked away from them, talking all the while.

"Hahaha, well, not yet!!! I've watched you guys, I know it's a short amount of time, but a lot has happened. I saw the pureness in you; your hearts felt good to me. I wasn't planning on doing this today, I wanted to get home, but since it's late, home will have to wait," said Skyla as she reached the outer part of the empty plot of land opposite Scott and Aegnor.

Scott watched as she then kneeled down, both knees on the ground. She reached around her back and, strainingly reached, moments later, pulled something out and placed it on the ground.

"Vwoooooooooommpp," the ground lit up, and a doorway opened.

4.

The Bunker

Scott watched as Skyla pulled the key back and placed it in her back.

He knew something big was about to happen and was holding in his excitement. He was quickly finding his way behind Skyla to follow her every step towards the doorway.

Aegnor followed, and all three walked in silence as they approached the doorway encased in white, like the rectangular box Scott was in at the prison. It just stood in this open plot of land in the middle of the forest, making a humming noise.

Standing in front of the doorway, between Aegnor and Scott, Skyla took their hands and pulled them forward through the doorway. Then they heard "phaaawaaump" and with a flash of light. All three stood in a room, brightly illuminated in a blueish-white glow.

Scott and Aegnor looked around; the walls seemed to display text and, in places, videos. There were glass counter cabinets all around them.

Skyla pulled both boys forward and turned around to face them.

She stood there in front of Scott and Aegnor, took a deep breath, reached around her back, the same spot she had earlier, and pulled out the key.

She was sure she was ready to share this story with them, but still, somewhere deep inside was a little hesitant. She had only just met them, but that feeling she had about them couldn't be ignored.

She took a deep breath again and started to speak. "I found this when I was a child. I was around 7 years old if I remember correctly. I had left my home in the afternoon to play towards the part of the river we were at just now, wandering around the forest looking at the animals. I always tried to catch them or get close enough to pet them and make friends with them.

I always wanted a pet, but my parents would not let me, saying that animals deserved to be free and that the forest was where they belonged, not in a house.

After a while, I finally reached the river and entered the water as I usually did, looking forward to feeling rejuvenated. As I moved around the water, I felt something on the bottom of my foot, and it felt like it had poked me. I looked down and around, carefully using my feet to move the crystals around, when I saw the edge of the object sticking out."

Scott and Aegnor watched, listening intently, waiting to hear the big thing they knew was coming.

"I reached down and grabbed it with my hands. The moment my fingers touched it, it started to glow. I could also hear a sound coming from all around me, as if the water and crystals were singing to me in a soft humming tone. I held it in my hands as I stood there in the river and kept getting this odd feeling running from the palm of my hand where the key was to the rest of my body.

I wanted to move and go back into the forest. I didn't know why; I just did. Something was compelling me to go, and so I did. The next thing I knew, it was as if I was in some sort of a trance; I was standing in the open spot in the woods where we just were. Again, as if instructed to do so, I walked to the outer edge of the barren plot of land, kneeled, and put the object into the ground, and the door appeared."

Skyla stared at Scott and Aegnor as they stared back in bewilderment.

Scott couldn't hold it in and blurted out in excitement, "So what is this place? What is that key?"

"I'm getting there, but now that you're here, I think it's just best you see for yourself," Skyla said as she made her way past the glass counter cabinets towards the back of the room, where there were 4 screens that seemed to just float there on the wall.

Scott and Aegnor followed, looking curiously at the objects through the glass.

"What are these things in the display?" Aegnor asked.

"Those are artifacts left behind by the Agatovians. I believe they are meant for us."

"What, why us?" Scott said.

"You will see," exclaimed Skyla, standing in front of the 4 screens at the back of the room.

Aegnor and Scott stood at her side, still in bewilderment and absolute anxiety, watching Skyla take the device out and place it in the console below the 4 floating screens.

The screens turned, and there in front of them was an alien standing in mid-air in front of the screens. It looked like it was made of pure light, a holographic image, and it started to speak.

"If you have found this place, then you have found a key bringing you here. Only you and the key holders are permitted to be here. The keys were made by us. We are the Agatovians.

They were created during a time of great divide on our planet between the Zarcovians and us.

We strived to develop and advance the universe in all aspects of life; food, agriculture, construction, technology, medicine, health, and many others.

In some cases, we developed the technology to provide such resources to the planet; in others, we discovered resources on the planet that enabled us to create or further our technology. It was through this we felt the universe has so much to offer. And so, this was our mission. Anything that we discovered we shared.

The Zarcovians look to dominate the universe, enslaving or killing anyone and anything in their way. They want to take the resources of other planets only to further themselves. On planets where resources are very high and widely scattered, they advance society, creating an efficient process for them to mine the resources. The locals, not being any wiser and having come from nothing, comply, living better lives but slowly killing off their own planet. Once the planet was dead, the Zarcovians would leave, letting whatever was living there die off.

As the Zarcovians ravaged more and more planets and our two races fought, we created a new device that would stop them from being able to portal.

Each device is encoded in the holder's blood. We were able to identify a specific genome only the Zarcovians had. The device was then used to destroy any device that had that genome through an intergalactic signal. This would stop any further travel and force any Zarcovian to stay where they were and blend into society.

This new device is called the "Crytivat" and is now the only key that can create a portal and many other things. It is like a crest in the shape of a hexagon and contains more power and technology than any of our past creations and something the Zarcovians know nothing about. We knew this would not be enough as we expected the Zarcovians to develop their own technology in time and begin rampaging the universe again. So we created 4 other keys that attach to the Crytivat that, when combined, provide the means to eradicate the Zarcovians.

You are now one of the key holders and must find the holder of the crest. You must find the other keys together, or the universe will end at the hands of the Zarcovians.

All the pieces of the key are scattered across the universe, as were both our people when our planet was destroyed."

As the recording continued to play, Scott and Aegnor stood with blank looks on their face.

"Save the what? Save the universe!!! Is that what that said?" Aegnor asked, looking a little pale.

He was, after all, the only person without a powerful key from some ancient civilization.

Scott looked over at him. "Yeah, I think that's what it said."

Skyla watched them both smirking. She felt more comfortable with everything going on. She did find and learn about the key when she was very young, so it did not frighten her. She was more excited than anything. This was an adventure, no, this was THE adventure she had waited for since she first got the key and heard the story. For years and years and years, she was waiting for something, now that something was standing there right before her.

The voice from the holographic image continued to speak, but now all three were looking at each other inquisitively, unable to hold their excitement about what to do next.

Scott and Aegnor blurted out, "So what do we do next?"

Skyla had already listened to the recording from the holographic Agatovian long ago, so she knew what had to be done next and could see the boys' excitement in their eyes.

"Well, we gotta find the other keys," she said, approaching Scott.

Standing in front of Scott with her key in hand, she slowly raised her hand to his chest, and it began to glow as she brought the key in contact with the Crytivat. As she opened her palm and let the key free, it floated as she pulled her hand away.

The key slowly attached itself to the right outer points of the Crytivats and made a humming sound as the Cyrtivat glowed even brighter. Then, as if appearing out of nowhere, something that looked like a mini Crytivat now floated in front of Scott's chest.

Skyla reached up and grabbed it quickly, pricking her finger as she did. She knew this would happen since the holographic message said they were encoded in blood, and each key holder would experience this.

"Wait, what, where, how did you do that?" asked Scott.

Skyla laughed sarcastically. "Well, if you guys listened to the message, you would know. I've seen it so many times that I thought it would be more fun if I just showed you. Now I have a key like you, and I'll be able to change into whatever species on the planet we end up on so we can blend in easier and go about our adventure."

Aegnor looked at them both with a lonely look on his face. "What… what about me?" he asked sadly.

"Well, when we find the next key, it will be all yours. In the meantime, there are a lot of cool gadgets here that you can equip yourself with. There's one that can change your face to the species on our planet. It was one of the Agatovians' earlier inventions before they figured out how to change the whole body. That way, you can blend in with us. Even though your body may differ, we can always dress you up to cover that part."

Aegnor said in a relieved tone, "Well, that makes me feel a whole lot better. At first, I thought, here we are going to different planets, and I'm going to stick out like a sore thumb, probably be the first to get eaten or captured."

Scott and Skyla burst out laughing.

"So what do we do next? How do we find the other keys? I mean, there has to be some sort of map or something," asked Scott

"Well, since the keys are lost, the only way to find them is through the Crytivat. Each key can only be found by the other keys. It's like they are linked together, programmed to find each other one by one as they come together. Now that the Crytivat has been found and has the first key, something should happen, but I've never done this, and the message only told me what I have shared with you. Maybe now that we have both keys, something will happen," Skyla said as she walked around the underground bunker.

Scott followed behind her while Aegnor circled the glass counter cabinets looking at the gadgets.

"Whoaaa, this is weird. What is it?" said Aegnor loudly as he looked at this object shaped like a half circle.

"I don't know. I have never touched any of the things in those cabinets. They actually never opened for me," Skyla said without looking.

"Ohh, I want it. It looks cool," said Aegnor with a smile on his face.

Skyla giggled and made her way to Aegnor, with Scott following.

As they approached the cabinet, there was a sound "Zawhooop, click-click," and the glass on the cabinet top seemed to disappear.

"Whoooaaa," exclaimed Skyla. "That's never happened. It must be because we now have 2 pieces, and the bunker is giving us access to more."

Aegnor was already reaching for the half-circle gadget lying there with one hand, grabbing a bunch of other stuff with the other, and putting them in his pocket.

51

"It's smooth and cold to the touch," said Aegnor, now holding it in his hand in front of him, running his fingers along the circular part of the gadget, then towards the flat side.

"Seeeeuhmmmmmpp," a bright arc shot out from the half circle part of the gadget into the wall, creating a bright flash blinding them all for a minute.

"What the heck was that!!!!" exclaimed Scott and Skyla simultaneously, looking at Aegnor.

Aegnor stood there with a dumbfounded look on his face but with a huge smile!

Seeing him like that, pointing at the wall with the gadget in his hands, Scott and Skyla figured out what had happened and smiled at each other.

Curious that the wall was still intact, they walked towards it. As they approached, it vanished, revealing a black square on the ground, like a void or something.

Aegnor ran up behind them, now being snapped out of the trance that he was in when the very wall he stood staring at vanished. "Whaooooooo!" he exclaimed.

"Ummm, please tell me we are not about to go in there," said Scott, remembering the last time he jumped into a black thing like that. He was riding an asteroid and was being taken to prison when he came back. It left a very unpleasant feeling in his stomach.

"I think we have to!!!" said Skyla in a courageous voice, grabbing them both by the hands and forward into pitch-black emptiness.

5.

A Brief History

"Noooooooooo," Skyla yelled

Aegnor and Scott had opened their eyes and looked in shock and horror.

In front of them, it looked like a war zone, fires burning in random spots; plant life destroyed, burned, trees split into pieces all over the place, smoke and the quiet sound of death all around them.

They stood there in disbelief and, almost as if instructed to do so, fell to their butts at the same time.

Skyla turns to Scott, tears on her cheeks. "What is going on, how is this…Our adventure just started! It just started! This isn't fair. How can it just end like this?!" she asked.

Scott put his hands over her shoulder and pulled her close, the other around Aegnor. "Our adventure did just start, and what's an adventure without a few obstacles," he said with a reassuring tone.

Feeling better, Skyla scrambled to her feet, trying to pull Scott and Aegnor up with her with no luck.

They both chuckled at first, making it a little hard for her, then got to their feet.

"What are we doing?" asked Scott as he watched her looking around the area, kicking debris away as she walked, brushing the rocks along the rock face with her hands as if looking for something.

Scott followed suit and started to do the same. "I'm not sure what you're looking for, but I'm going to help look, too. Any chance you can share what I am looking for would be great."

Skyla chuckled. "Come here, next to me, and let's search together; I have a feeling that if anything is going to happen, it will be when we are together like it did in the bunker before we came to this place."

They walked in unison along the rock face feeling around, listening, looking for anything. At first, they didn't think they found anything until Aegnor yelled out, "Stop!!!!! Don't move, don't you hear that, that buzzing, humming sound that seems to crackle occasionally."

Excited, Scott and Skyla put their bodies closer to the semi-destroyed rock surface wall and moved along slower till they heard and felt it. "Yeah, we hear it too; we can also feel it now," said Skyla as she backed away to look for anything.

Aegnor to his left, Scott now stood back, all three scanning for something.

"Wait, I see something," says Scott excitedly, jumping forward into the rubble wall, starting to clear away the rocks.

After just a moment, Skyla and Aegnor could see what Scott saw, it was light coming from underneath the rubble, and they both jumped in to help Scott.

After a few moments, they uncovered a glowing white doorway, which was very similar to the one in the forest on Skyla's planet.

Skyla proceeded through the doorway. Scott and Aegnor knowing what to expect, confidently followed.

Like a blip, all three now stood in what looked like a war room, digital maps floating in the air, walls, and rooms filled with weapons, tech, clothing, etc…

"Whooaaaaaa, this is a war room," exclaimed Aegnor, having seen the prisons, he remembered seeing similar rooms. And started off looking at everything that was around him.

Scott and Skyla looked around and then, as if they telepathically agreed to do so, walked towards the back wall with 4 screens on it, and as they approached, the walls, screens, and displays all lit up a bit brighter. Then suddenly, in front of the four screens, the Agatovian holographic image appeared and began to speak.

"Welcome, Crytivat and Key holders. If you are here, it means the Crytivat and the "kryasia" key have been brought together.

Long ago, we prophesized the Zagatovians would take over the universe at some point and created the means to stop it. You are those means...

The Keys are designed with one of our fundamentals of Unity – They are intended to work together, only then being at their strongest. The key holder who gives the key to the Crytivat holder receives a smaller crytivat, which has most of the same capabilities and 1 unique power.

Now you must find the remaining keys so we can activate the device and stop the Zarcovians once and for all.

Together is the only way to win!!!

Behind you, on those maps, you will see we are tracking the keys, and the location of the second key will only reveal itself when there are two Crytivats present."

Just as they were looking, they turned their bodies and approached the maps, completely ignoring the talking Agatovian.

A blue light got brighter as they approached the map.

"Well, that seemed pretty straightforward, so where are we?" asked Scott looking at a map of the universe in awe.

"That's weird, the map says we are on Yarsova and that the key is here as well, but when we got here, it was all destroyed outside as far as I could see," said Skyla as she carefully studied the map.

"Well, I guess the adventure starts. We have to go and find the next key… wait a second, um, how will we find the next key? Where do we even start?" asked Scott. "When we found each other, it was by chance!!!"-

"I'm not really sure, maybe something will happen as we get closer," said Skyla looking at Scott.

"Ummmmm, guys. I need a little help," shouted Aegnor

They both looked over to see Aegnor in a room, hanging in some sort of suit that was being held up by some type of machine arms that were connected to what looked like a computer station.

"What the… What did you do? How did you get stuck in that thing, hanging?" asked Scott as he and Skyla walked over to the room.

"I can't wait to hear this!!!" said Skyla laughingly

"I don't know, I just walked into this room and saw this cool-looking suit hanging there and wanted to take a closer look. As I walked towards it, the floor rose or something because I was right in front of it. At this point, I had to try it on, so well, I um, I tried it on, and then the floor just disappeared from under me, and I was still attached to these arms. Can you look at that station over there, please? Maybe it has some controls or interface." Aegnor explained.

Skyla giggled as she made her way with Scott to what now looked like a computer station with screens floating and a terminal type of interface below against a wall.

"Whoaaa, that's crazy, it looked like a solid wall from the other side, and from here, you can see right through it," said Scott excitedly. He was still blown away by all the cool things he continued to see.

"Ok, well... hold on. Hmmm, wait. Yeah yeah – ok – yeah, that's it, I got it," shouted Skyla. She tapped a few more times on the terminal.

"Aahhhhhhhh!" screamed Aegnor as he fell to the ground, which was just three feet from where he was.

"What is this suit I'm wearing?" Aegnor asked as he got to his feet and made his way to Scott and Skyla.

"Well, according to what I'm reading, it's a suit that will transform you to whatever species planet we are on... Oh wait, this must be the rest of the one that's back at my bunker that changes your head," said Skyla.

Aegnor was visibly excited on his toes, bouncing from one foot to the other.

"Wow, this is so cool!!! Now I really feel like I'm part of the gang," said Aegnor

Skyla and Scott smiled and started to walk back toward the maps. Aegnor followed behind, looking down at his suit as he stumbled forward.

"Oh wait, Skyla, I grabbed a bunch of stuff from the cabinet when I was checking out the arc thing. You think there's any chance I grabbed it," said Agenor as he reached into his pocket and pulled out a palm full of small to medium size devices.

Skyla turned around and looked down at Aegnor's hands, and to her surprise, there was a circular blueish sliver-colored object.

"Wow, yeah, that is, that's the one, the circular one! What are the chances of that?!" said Skyla excitedly.

Aegnor picked the object out of his hand, and as he brought it closer, it flew out of his hands and floated in front of his chest, the suit's chest, and then it vanished, and the suit glowed for a moment, and Aegnor felt a gentle jolt and sensation from the base of his neck to his head.

"Whoaaa, yeah, totally felt something there. I feel more complete; it's like I was missing something before like the suit wanted the head. I feel stronger too." said Aegnor

Skyla smiled at Aegnor, then looked at Scott with a different kind of smile and grabbed his hands, pulling him back towards the maps. Aegnor quickly followed.

"Maybe there's something on these walls or in these cabinets that can help," said Scott as he looked around carefully, although he didn't really know what he was looking for.

He then came across a set of bracelets that had two crest-shaped objects opposite each other and seemed to glow as he went to touch them. Fascinated and curious, he proceeded to place a bracelet on each hand.

"Wooooooomp!" sounded from Scott as he glowed brightly.

"Whooooaaaaa, that was incredible. I feel strong, full of energy," said Scott loudly.

"What are you guys doing?" asked Skyla as she made her way over to them.

"Well, I put these bracelets on, and I feel amazing. There's another set here, come closer, so I can put them on you," said Scott with a smile on his face.

Skyla stopped dead in her tracks, blushing for a moment, giggled, walked closer, and put her arms out.

Scott put the bracelets on Skyla, and there was a "Whooooomp!" as she glowed brightly for a moment

"Whooooooaaaa yeah, that was amazing," shouted Skyla.

"Are there any more bracelets?" asked Aegnor.

"No, sorry, Aegnor, that was the last one," said Scott.

"Oh man," sighed Aegnor.

"Ok, boys, we got to find something that we can use to track the key," said Skyla as she turned and continued to look.

Scott started looking again and came across another device, shaped like a square with two points on the left and right or top and bottom, depending on which way you looked at it. He reached to grab it, and it started to buzz slightly on his fingertips. As he brought it closer to his eyes to take a closer look, his hand passed in front of his chest, and the device flew out of his fingers and floated in front of his chest, then disappeared into the crest, sending a tingly feeling around his chest, down his neck to between his shoulder blades and then it was gone.

"That was weird," said Scott.

"What," said Skyla and Aegnor at the same time.

"Nothing really, I mean, I touched this thing, a device, I guess, and when I took it to look at it, it disappeared into my chest. I felt a little tingle, then it was gone," said Scott.

"I think everything in here is awesome and meant to be here for us, so it can't be bad, right," said Aegnor.

All three of them nodded approvingly and continued to search for something that would help them find the next key.

Aegnor then came across a cabinet with what looked like a bracelet, but for the arm, an armlet, it was a shiny blueish silver color, about six to eight inches long on display. He reached down, grabbed it, and placed it on his arm, but nothing happened. He moved his other hand along the device, feeling for a button or something to turn it on.

"Oh man, what the heck? This thing won't turn on. Why won't this turn on?" said Aegnor, slightly frustrated.

Hearing this, Skyla and Scott turned and walked towards Aegnor.

"What happened? What's going on? What did you do?" asked Skyla, jokingly accusing him.

Scott chuckled at the way Skyla asked.

"Nothing, I swear, there were a few of these armlets on display, so I took one, put it on, but nothing happened," said Aegnor defensively.

Skyla and Scott stood in front of the cabinet display, each reached down to grab an armlet, and as they got closer, they started to glow. They both placed the armlets on their arms, and then the devices tightened, glowing brightly for a moment.

"What, oh come on, is that only for you guys?" Aegnor exclaimed.

Skyla and Scott chuckled as they examined the armlet device.

"Whoaaa guys, a screen just popped up on my armlet! But it's blank!" exclaimed Scott.

"How did you do that" asked Skyla, turning to face Scott.

"I just ran my hand over the top of it," said Scott.

"I got it, thanks! My screen's blank too. Hmmm, I wonder...follow me," said Skyla as she walked back towards the floating maps with the locations of the keys, the next one being the brightest.

As they stood in front of the maps, their armlets glowed for a moment, and then all of a sudden, they were seeing the same thing as the maps floating above their arms.

"That's it, just as I thought! The closer we got to the maps, the armlets would sync up or something! Now our adventure starts!!!" said Skyla excitedly.

Aegnor spoke loudly, "What adventure? I don't have any maps. What if I get lost or something? How would I ever find my way? The adventure will then be you finding my dead body somewhere because of some animal or …."

"Whoooaaaaa, calm down. Hold on a sec…" said Skyla as she approached him and placed her armlet next to his. There was a light glow, and the map appeared.

"Just as I thought! When I saw multiple armlets, I figured there had to be a way after Scott and mine started working. My guess was once the key holders activate it, then they can activate others. Now look, and you can see we show up on each other's maps. Look, the key is blue, I'm white, Aegnor is red, and Scott, you're yellow."

"Now the adventure really begins!!!!" Aegnor laughed, feeling better knowing he wouldn't be left behind to be eaten or something.

They all chuckled loudly as they walked back the way they entered, through the wall to stare at a burnt fire-ridden barren land as far as they could see.

Almost as though trained to do so, all of them raised their armlet arms, ran their hands across the top, and looked at the map.

"Cool, but yeah, I have no idea what I'm looking for, so who's got this," said Aegnor bluntly.

"I got it. Let me explain…"

Scott was also a little bewildered at what he was looking at. All he knew was what the color dots were.

He was glad Aegnor said he didn't know what he was looking at. He got a little closer to listen and watched as Skyla explained how the map worked and was laid out. Although extremely complex, it was somehow easy for Scott to break it down to our Cardinal directions of North, East, South, and west, at least while on land.

"So to keep it simple, make sure our dots are all together and that the blue dot is in front of us at all times."

"Ahhh, that I can understand," said Aegnor proudly.

They all chuckled and started to walk towards the gratsani glowing in blue.

6.

Kreynak

"I don't know what happened here, but it must have been bad, like someone dropped a gazillion bombs," said Scott as he smelled the burnt Earth around him, being careful not to step anywhere that was still on fire.

They all walked for some time; it was dark, and the barren, burnt land was seemingly never-ending.

"Is there anything at all left on this planet? We have been walking forever, and it's still the same; burnt, on fire, stinky," said Aegnor as he walked, huffing and puffing heavily.

"Wait, Scott. What are we doing, you remember what we did when we were in prison on Aegnor's planet, and I told you to think of somewhere safe and hit your chest. I think we can do the same here. Look as far as you can, pick a point in your sight that you want to be at and hit your chest." said Skyla.

Scott's eyes opened wide. "Oh yeah, I completely forgot. Wait, I think you can do it to Skyla, you have a crytivat."

Scott looked at his map and peered into the distance, squinting his yellowish-red eyes.

"Ahhh, ok, Skyla, look over there, see that tall burning tree just past that black rock?" asked Scott.

"Hmmm, no, not really… hold on," said Skyla as she walked up behind him, got up on the tips of her feet, and rested her head on his shoulders.

Scott froze for a minute, unable to concentrate with Skyla's head on his shoulders and their cheeks touching.

"Ohhh ahhh! Ummm...Yeah... so if you look down my arm towards my finger, you will see the burning tree and to the right, the black rock," said Scott.

The more time they spent together, the closer and closer he felt to her, she had saved his life after all and was a key holder. Scott felt he had a strong friendship with her, but those feelings were starting to grow.

Skyla pushed her face closer to Scott's and placed her arm alongside his, and squinted her eyes, "Yeah, I see it now!!!"

Skyla jumped to the side, eyes set on her target, and without a word, hit her chest, "Whooooooomp", and just like that, she was gone.

"What...What the heck? Did she just portal? All by herself? She's crazy, she didn't even see the spot till you showed her, and she just "whoomps" over there no warning, I mean, what If something jumps out and kills her before we get there, I swear this girl is gonna get us ki...."

"Yeah, she's great!!!" said Scott as he grabbed Aegnor's hand, hit his chest, and portaled to Skyla.

"Hey guys, how was the ride? What took you so long!!! I had to try the portal thing, I just couldn't wait," said Skyla excitedly.

"You're crazy, you know that!" exclaimed Aegnor, laughing.

"Ok, now we know this works, we just keep doing it till we see something," said Scott.

"Oh, thank God it worked, I don't know how much longer I could keep going," said Aegnor.

"Yeah, this is great! Ok, you guys ready for the next jump," said Scott.

"My turn to pick!" shouted Skyla and ran up to Scott, grabbed both his hands, and lifted his arms up and over her shoulders, her back now against his chest.

Scott stood there like a puppet on strings as she manipulated his arms over her shoulders and ended up with her warm cheek against his.

Aegnor stood close to them both, his shoulder against Scott's.

"Now, look over my arm towards my finger, see where I'm pointing, see that...."

"Whack...Whoooooomp."

"Haahahaaahaa," laughed Skyla as they arrived at the spot she had her eyes on.

"What the heck was that? I mean...Seriously...a warning...what if I wasn't touching either of you, I would have been left behi...."

"Oh, come on, Aegnor, that was fun!" said Scott, interrupting Aegnor's rant.

"Yeah, fine.. it was," said Aegnor with a smirk.

"I figured we could try to make this fun since there doesn't seem to be an end in sight, having said that, Aegnor, it's your turn," said Skyla looking out into the distance.

"Oh sweet, ok...I got this. Ok, oh, this one's good, see that bright flame, almost shines like a star from here, it's between that light and the...you know what, both of you come here behind me and put your heads on my shoulders and look where both my hands meet and point. Do you see it?" asked Aegnor.

"Yeah, we see it..."

"Whack!"

"Whoooooomp!"

"Whoooaaaaaa!" shouted Aegnor as he lost his footing and slipped off the edge of the cliff.

Skyla and Scott shouted "Aegnor" as they both jumped forward, landing on their bellies at the edge of the cliff. "Aegnor, are you ok?"

"Yeah, you know, just um, hanging around. This would count as fun, right Skyla" said Aegnor as he held on tightly to the cliff's edge.

"Oh my God, Aegnor, come here, grab our hands!" shouted Skyla, her voice noticeably shaken by what happened.

Scott and Skyla grabbed Aegnor's hands and pulled him up onto the ground. Aegnor laid there for a moment on his belly and slowly turned over and sat up, holding his knees.

"What the heck happened?" asked Aegnor.

"I don't know, but whatever it was, you got us here, look, there's a whole city down there," said Skyla as she looked down into the dark and seemingly deep canyons.

They all looked out and saw lights in various configurations nicely aligned all over the place and in bunches throughout the darkness that lay beyond the cliff. They seemed to go endlessly downwards from the top of the cliff, some were long belts of lights, while some were a combination of squares, rectangles and large ovals, and others stood solitary in the darkness. There were strings of lights that seemed to go from one end of the darkness to another.

"I can't see much, but It looks like it's going to be daytime soon, then we can figure out how to get down there!" said Scott.

"What's daytime?" asked Aegnor and Skyla.

Scott explained, "Oh, yeah… So, where I'm from Earth; we have a Moon and a Sun, the Sun is a star that was created 4.5 billion years ago, it's what provides light and heat for us to survive. The Earth rotates, so around every 12hrs or so, the Sun sets, and the Moon rises, bringing night."

"What are hours?" they both asked again.

"Oh boy, so the time for Earth to make a full rotation is 24hrs, each hour is made of 60minutes, and each minute is made up of 60 secs," said Scott as he looked at Aegnor and Skyla staring at him blankly.

"Whoa, let's just stick with light out or dark out, I have no idea what you're talking about," said Aegnor.

They all chuckled loudly as night became day. They looked out into the deep canyons, stretching as far as the eye could see, weaving in and out of the mountains. The lights they saw before floating in the darkness now showed structures that lined the mountains in the same way the lights were arranged at night. Some were embedded into the canyon walls, others jutted out, connecting to either another structure or connected to long walkways or rails that spanned from one canyon wall to another.

"What are those little things flying around? You guys see those little black things that look like they are moving around," asked Scott.

"Yeah, I don't know can't really tell what they are from here. Maybe some flying creature that will eat us or maybe its some kinda ship," said Aegnor.

"Why do you always think something is going to eat us?" asked Skyla laughingly.

"Hahaha, I don't know, maybe because we keep portaling to these unknown places. What if we do it and end up in the nest of a Carnivacs or something?" replied Aegnor.

"Carnivacs?" asked Scott and Skyla.

"Oh yeah, those things are bad, they have 4 legs, kinda scaly, then they have another four legs with poison claws at the ends and have these long necks and ears that are like tentacles, and they have rows of big sharp teeth with 4 tongues that take the prey in after it has been struck by the claws and…"

"Okay, okay, we get it," chuckled Scott and Skyla.

"Now we have to figure out how to get down there, the blue light on the maps shows it's somewhere down there," said Scott as he started looking around.

"I see something, look over there, it's like a door!" shouted Skyla.

"I see it, I see it," said Aegnor.

"Okay, well, let's get to it," said Scott, and they all started walking along the cliff edge, looking down into the canyons at the beautiful city within it.

As the morning progressed, it got brighter out, and they started to see creatures flying through the air just at the top of the canyon where they were walking.

There were a variety of them flying around, one in particular caught Scott's eye. It was a long orange-eared, reddish green furry thing with a stout black nose, like a pig, four long skinny legs, a tail that split into three about midway and the weird part was it had a helicopter-type wing thing on its back which looked like it was what made the creature fly.

Skyla stopped as she was walking, looking into the canyon. "Ohhhh, look at that, it's so beautiful."

"What?" asked Scott and Aegnor.

Skyla pointed out into the canyon, closer to the side they were on. "Look, see that serpent-faced, red fire-colored creature flying over there, yellow stripe from its head to the tails, long neck, huge wings, and long wide tail!!!"

"Oh yeah, that is beautiful!" said Scott confirming Skyla's idea of beauty.

"Oh yeah, sure, beautiful now, till it wants to eat you!!!" shouted Aegnor.

Skyla and Scott laughed as they all continued walking towards the solitary door-like object that stood just a bit further ahead.

As they stepped in front of the large glowing door, a voice came from it in an alien language which everyone was able to translate since they all had alien tech. "Welcome to Yarsova, please step through to enter the city."

"Wow, that's pretty cool!" said Scott, astonished by what he saw.

Skyla grabbed Scott and Aegnor's hands and pulled them forward into the door.

"I mean, seriously, Skyla, do you ever stop and think just a moment before you do things," asked Aegnor, slightly relieved there was no danger on this side of the portal door.

"Not really, where's the fun in that?" chuckled Skyla as she took Scott's arm and wrapped it around hers.

They all stood and looked out into the city that lined the walls of the canyon, watching balls of light zipping above on floating bridges spanning from one side to the other. They felt so small looking up to the top of the canyon. In front of them were streets lined with a few aliens and what looked like shops, places to eat, street carts and other things. It was still early, and it looked like the city was just waking up.

"Wow!" exclaimed Skyla. "I've never seen anything like this, look at this place!"

"Yeah, this is definitely the coolest place I have ever seen!" agreed Scott.

"Yeah, very cool. Do you guys smell that? I don't know what it is, but it smells so good, and I am starving. This is the last time we are back at my house," said Aegnor, already walking in the direction of the smell.

"Now that you mention it, yeah! I'm starving," said Skyla pulling Scott forward, still holding his arm in hers.

Scott didn't feel so shy anymore with Skyla, he liked being close to her now and was right by her side following Aegnor.

"Yeah, that does smell good!" confirmed Scott, thinking to himself that it was weird he felt this way. He was human after all, but what he had at Aegnor's house, even though it didn't look appetizing, turned out to be quite delicious, and right now, he was starving.

"I think we are getting closer," said Aegnor.

Scott chuckled, watching Aegnor, quietly whispering to Skyla that he looked like a hound dog hunting a fox, which of course led to the inevitable explanation of what a fox and hound dog was, although since they are in the same family of animal, it was a little easier.

"We're here! This is it!" said Aegnor walking through the entrance of what looked like a restaurant.

"Jeez, Aegnor, we almost lost you," said Scott, but didn't see Aegnor in front of him when they came through the entrance.

"Can I get some help over here?" shouted Aegnor from the side.

"Hahahahhaa, you really are hungry, aren't you!!!" laughed Skyla looking to the side at Aegnor, already sitting at a table, staring down at what looked like a menu. She started walking towards Aegnor, still holding Scott's arm. Once they got to the booth-like table, she bumped Scott with her hip, forcing him into the booth and sat next to him, across from Aegnor.

"Hello, can I get some help here please!!!" shouted Aegnor.

"You already know what you want to get? I don't know what I'm looking at!" said Scott as he stared down at the table, which had a shiny black finish in which the menus seemed to just float.

"I haven't the slightest, all I know is I'm getting whatever I'm smelling."

"Definitely agree with you there," laughed Skyla.

Just then, an alien approached their table, it had black matte and shiny scales, with lines of magenta woven into the black, and a long nose that seemed to come to a hook-type end, although not so sharp and curved and had ovalish eyes that stood vertically on their face. It looked like they were looking at the oddly, although they really couldn't be sure since it was the first time seeing this alien.

"Um, hi, ahh, how can I help you," asked a soft male voice.

"Hi, yes, I want whatever I'm smelling, what is that," asked Aegnor.

"Oh, that's fresh "siisiiriktak", it should be ready in just a few minutes. It's one of the best dishes," said the waiter.

"Oh ok, but um, what is it, like what is it?" asked Aegnor.

Scott was watching as the waiter looked back at Aegnor with a blank face as if he should know this and was just being a pain in the butt and making him tell them the ingredients.

"Ughhhh, well, it is a mix of siisii, rik and tak, so you get a little of the land, air and liquid living creatures in one tasty dish with a homemade sauce made from ingredients grown right here," explained the waiter.

Aegnor began to ask, "What are sii…"

Scott interrupted, "Yes, yes, we will take 3 siisiiriktak."

"Aegnor… were locals remember, were supposed to know what foods are what around here, we gotta be careful. If we act like this, we will give ourselves away," said Scott quietly, leaning over the table closer to Aegnor.

"Oh shoot, yeah yeah, you're right, sorry I was just so hungry I couldn't think straight," said Aegnor apologetically.

"Totally get it, Aegnor, I would have done the same. I can't wait to eat," said Skyla.

Scott watched as they nodded in agreement, he could see Aegnor was happy to hear that Skyla would have done the same. He felt Aegnor was feeling a little left out because of the way Skyla had been jumping into everything without discussion, dragging them with her without thinking. He thought, as with any relationship, you had to look past the small things. He could see that was happening, and they were bonding.

"Have you guys looked at the map since we got here?" asked Scott.

"Not a chance I was on the hunt for the food, hahaha," laughed Aegnor.

Skyla chuckled and scooched closer to Scott, put her arm over his shoulders and hunched him over with her so they created a shield with their bodies so no one could see in and pulled the map up under the table.

"It looks like it's a bit deeper into the city," said Scott.

"Yeah, but it doesn't seem too far if you look at how long it took to get here from where we were. See, we were here before, and it took about ten minutes to get here, so I'm thinking double that should get us to the key, assuming it stays wherever it is," said Skyla.

"Hello, three fresh, hot siisiiriktak. Please be careful with your hands, the plates are hot. You didn't ask for anything to drink, so I brought some fresh "kratla" which was picked this morning and freshly squeezed, please enjoy your meal," said the waiter.

"Ohhhhh, yes yes yes, that smells sooooo good!" cried Aegnor as he grabbed something to eat with and started shoving handfuls of food into his mouth.

Skyla and Scott laughed, watching Aegnor and quickly joined him, shoving food in their mouths. They ate in silence until their plates were empty.

"Man, that was good. I mean, I was starving, so anything would be good, but that was really good!" said Aegnor as he sat back and rubbed his belly.

"Yeah, totally agree," confirmed Scott, also sitting back and relaxing, having finished his food around the same time as Aegnor.

Skyla also confirmed, food in her mouth, smiling, "Mmhh yaa, mhhh, so good, mmhh!!!"

Aegnor and Scott laughed, watching her enjoy the food and drinking the fresh kratla.

"Wow, this kratla is delicious, it's so sweet, kinda creamy and has these little crunchy bits in it," said Scott.

"Wow, yea, that's amazing," confirmed Skyla.

Aegnor nodded in agreement, still drinking his kratla.

"Ummm guys, I didn't even think about this till just now, but, ummm… how are we gonna pay for this." asked Scott lowering his voice as is got to pay.

Just then, as if appearing out of thin air, the waiter stood at the table, "Hi, I hope you enjoyed your meal, will there be anything else I can serve you today?"

"No, I think we are good, can we get the check, please?" asked Skyla, reaching back into her compartment in her body.

"Whoaa Whoaa Whoaaa, I got this, guys!" exclaimed Aegnor.

"You got what? Where did you get money from?" asked Scott.

"Didn't you look in the pack that my dad gave us? There was a bunch of stuff in there, like survival stuff. Small hunting knives, snacks, communication devices, etc.… and money."

"I totally forgot about that with everything going on, I never opened mine. I left it at the bunker at Skyla's place, where did you even have time to… never mind," said Scott and laughed.

"Yeah, same here. Well then, thank you so much for feeding us such a wonderful meal this morning," said Skyla smiling warmly at Aegnor.

Scott watched as Aegnor paid the bill and still managed to have a good amount of money left over, he was happy that eating did not cost too much as there was money left over.

They all stood up and made their way towards the exit of the restaurant, thanking them for a wonderful meal on their way out.

The streets are more alive now with aliens bustling around busy, each with their own agenda, as always somewhere to go, something to do.

Scott looked at how lively it had become since they first got here and thought to himself, this is how it looks on Earth, in any city, streets full of people running around, heads down, on a mission to get where they need to get, some shopping, some eating at the carts that looked abandoned earlier and others just hanging out.

"We gotta go this way, guys, come on," said Skyla, leading the way down the road. "There are a few more bends in the road we have to get past. Then we should be close."

They all walked together, looking at the various places along the way.

"Hey guys, um… have you noticed that everyone has been staring at us?" said Aegnor.

"No, sorry, I wasn't paying attention, just so full, trying to walk," laughed Scott as he watched the native aliens watching him and huddling in groups as they passed.

"Oh yeah, that's super weird," said Skyla. "Let's pick up the pace. Hopefully, there won't be as many people the further we get from the entrance."

"Aegnor, Skyla, keep walking and listen. Look at yourself real quick and look at them, notice anything."

"What the? Oh, this can't be good! Why don't we look like them? What the heck is going on?!" exclaimed Aegnor in panic.

Skyla was raised, and a firm but a calm voice said, "Ok, ok, ok, it's ok, come hurry, there looks to be a little road or something that cuts off the main road."

They all moved quickly into what looked like an alleyway but was made by the natural winds that blew through the canyon. It seemed to go far into the canyon and gave enough coverage that they wouldn't be seen from the street.

Skyla looked at everyone. "Ok, so yeah, that was weird, why do we look like this, and they look like that? Who are they? What happened to aliens that looked like us? I'm a little scared, and I don't know what to do?"

Scott was resting with his back against the canyon wall, he leaned forward and took Skyla's hands in his, "Skyla, it's ok, you don't HAVE to know what to do, we are a team, all here together, we can figure this out. Not sure if you noticed, but all the other aliens were doing was staring and talking. It didn't look like anyone was doing anything about it. We haven't been captured. I didn't feel threatened. Haven't heard any alarm..."

Skyla replied, looking a little calmer now. "You're right, you're right. We are ok, so far! It is odd but doesn't seem hostile. Let's proceed with caution, maybe on less traveled roads. Not sure where this alleyway goes, but let's find out. The map says it's in that direction anyways, maybe we get lucky, and this is shorter."

Skyla started walking along the narrow walkway carved in the canyon walls by the winds, and Scott and Aegnor followed. Along the way, at times, they had to walk sideways and on the walls to get over a spot that somehow was untouched by the winds. They walked for a while, not encountering anyone along the way, which showed in their noticeably calm faces.

"I think I see an end," shouts Aegnor. "Just around the next corner, I saw a peek of light when I ran up the wall just now."

"Why were you running… never mind…" laughed Skyla. "Yeah, the map's showing this direction too, so we got lucky taking this route."

"Whoaaa, look at that, how is that here? I would have never guessed something like this would be here," exclaimed Scott, now overlooking a lush forest nestled in the canyons.

7.

Devastation

"Wow, amazing," confirmed Skyla as she pulled up the map on her arm, "Map says it's down there, straight ahead. We should keep a weapon in our hands. Not all forests are like the one on my planet, and not all creatures are friendly."

"I'm ok with that, definitely don't want to get eaten by anything," exclaimed Aegnor as he started reaching into his pack to grab his arc light device that he found at the bunker on Skyla's planet.

"Oh boy, that thing again," laughed Scott, "Let's be a little more careful with that thing this time."

"Hahaha yeah, I hear ya," laughed Aegnor.

They all started making their way down from the alley they were in into the lush forest below.

Scott walked, careful not to slip on his way down, occasionally grabbing Skyla or Aegnor's hands to avoid falling.

"Definitely nothing like this on Earth," exclaimed Scott, now in the cover of the forest. Most of the foliage around him were large tentacle-like trunks of a tree with arc-shaped leaves that were illuminated in different colors and had bright highlighter kind of colors along the outer edge of the leaf. He noticed little insect-type creatures walking up and down the tree and along the leaves, and down the trunk like a marching band carrying bits of the tree.

It was interesting to Scott to see that even though he was on another planet, life was very similar. The smallest of creatures had a function, operated by a law that spanned the universe.

"Ahhhhhh, did you guys see that? I just saw something run through the bushes over there to the right," yelled Aegnor.

"See what?" Scott asked.

"Is your mind playing tricks on you, Aegnor?" asked Skyla.

"No, no, I swear I saw something run through over there," confirmed Aegnor.

"Ok, well, keep your weapons handy and eyes open," said Skyla.

Scott didn't have any weapons, he just knew that his suit did things that he still didn't know how to activate or control. He guessed it could sense danger and equip as necessary as it did back in prison. He tried to stay focused but found himself paying more attention to the creatures that were running around, sometimes right between his feet. There were these little balls of hair and bright yellow eyes with pointy ears and he guessed the legs must be somewhere underneath the ball of hair somewhere. Scott thought they were kind of cute.

"Right there, right there, look, hurry!" shouted Aegnor.

Scott looked up, hearing Aegnor's voice, "Yeah, I think I saw it too. It was over there to that side."

"Ok, ok, guys, stay focused we gotta keep moving in the direction the map is pointing, and the last time I checked, it was that way," exclaimed Skyla as she brought up the map. "See, it says it right... wait, it changed. Which way did you guys say you saw something?" asked Skyla.

"Over there to the right," confirmed Aegnor and Scott at the same time.

"Do you think whatever we keep seeing has the second key?" asked Aegnor.

"Well, for now, I'm gonna have to say it's entirely possible," confirmed Skyla.

"It's probably some alien-eating monster that ate the key and will probably eat us too," noted Aegnor seriously.

"Hahaha, you and your getting eaten all the time. Did you get attacked or something when you were a kid?" asked Scott. He knew, sometimes people had trauma from their childhood that often lasted a lifetime.

"Nope, I just think anything with sharp teeth that can eat me will eat me," said Aegnor.

"Bahahahahaa," laughed Skyla. "That is an interesting way to look at it."

"Ha ha ha, you won't be laughing when half your foot is gone because something bit it off," said Aegnor defensively.

"Ok, ok, you two, let's get moving and keep an eye on your map," said Scott with his map up, walking in the direction of the blue dot. "If this thing really has our key and is some creature running around with it, then it will be moving."

They all continued walking, eyes open, watching, side by side, they could see a little over 180 degrees.

"We are getting close, just a bit more, and we should be at the key," said Skyla "We need to be real quiet, if it's a creature or something, we don't want to scare it away."

"Or give it a chance to eat us!!!" chimed Aegnor.

They all chuckled softly, careful not to scare off anything. They walked towards the blue dot on the map. As they got closer, they found themselves at the top of a slight hill, looking down on what looked like a small village. There were at least 5 or 6 huts lined up next to each other, not too close, it looked like a comfortable amount of space around each hut, almost as though each one had its own plot of land or yard that was meant only for that hut. They could see aliens going about their business below, and little ones running around playing, throwing something and little creatures running about chasing whatever was thrown, some looked to be small children aliens, and some looked to be about the same age or at least the same size as Scott.

"Well, the key is definitely down there, but it's moving a lot," said Skyla, "which is weird 'cause the movements don't match what we see down there, we gotta get closer. Do you see that third hut? Just behind it looks like there's some thick foliage that we can probably hide in."

"Should we wait until it's dark to start going down there?" asked Scott.

"I think we can make it down there now; we seem to have pretty good coverage till there if we stay behind the bushes and trees," said Skyla and started walking down the hill.

Scott and Aegnor followed, they both felt Skyla knew way more than either of them did. Aegnor had never seen any of the places or things that they had been to so far, he was born and raised on Scarsavo and had never seen more than where he lived or the underground city. They did not have to go too far and reached the spot behind the third hut quickly and sat down.

"Okay, let's hang out here till the key stops moving all over the place," said Skyla as she watched the village through the bushes, trying to figure out what was going on with the key and how it could move so quickly.

"Yeah, I could use a little break," said Aegnor as he went down to sit, then suddenly, his foot slipped out from underneath him, and he tumbled backward over the bushes and rolled down the rest of the hill till he slammed up against the third hut.

"Aegnor!!!" shouted Skyla and Scott at the same time, jumping to their feet, not realizing how loud they had yelled.

Just then, all the aliens stopped and looked over at them standing behind the bush and started walking towards them.

"Oh no, this is not good," said Scott.

"No, it is not, and no point in hiding now, let's go check on Aegnor and make sure he's ok," said Skyla.

They both made their way to Aegnor, and the aliens were making their way towards him as well.

"Aegnor, are you ok? That fall looked pretty bad," said Skyla, as she reached down to grab his hands and help him to his feet.

Scott quickly joined her and grabbed Aegnor's other hands, and they all stood there watching as the aliens approached them.

"How are you here? You are not supposed to be here," said the elderly alien that looked to be leading the group, which looked like the entire village, including the kids.

"I don't understand, we are from here, why wouldn't we be allowed to roam freely," asked Skyla.

"You do not understand, hurry up, come with me so no one can see that you're here, come, hurry!" said the elderly alien.

Scott, Skyla and Aegnor followed quietly and entered the hut behind the elderly alien and a handful of the other aliens, the entire village could not fit in that hut.

"The rest of you, stay outside and do what you normally do, do not talk about the visitors, just go about your regular business," said the elderly alien to the rest of the aliens. They all dispersed quietly, whispering to each other.

"No whispering!" shouted the elderly alien.

Scott and Skyla chuckled under their breath while Aegnor stood there still as a board.

"Come sit," said the elderly alien, "what I am going to tell you is not something you want to stand for."

"What's going on here? Why are we the only aliens that look like this? This is our home planet, where did our kind go?" asked Skyla.

"Oh, my dear, I'm sorry, but your kind are no more, after the leaders were done taking all that they needed for this planet, they destroyed all the underground facilities while your people were still there," said the elderly alien.

"That's horrible, who are these leaders? Are they the Zarcovians?" asked Skyla.

"My dear, yes, they are the Zarcovians, we are also Zarcovians," said the elderly alien.

"Wait! What? You are Zarcovians, then why are you still here? Why wouldn't you leave with your kind?" asked Skyla.

"My dear, the Zarcovian race had split over the centuries. As we evolved, there was a group that was trying to make the race stronger, live longer, and less susceptible to the elements of the various planets that they wished to conquer, in doing so, the leader race evolved, and they enslaved anyone that was not in the same race, including their own people. So we were forced to work with the native race of the planet, building the facilities to mine the resources and organizing the natives to work according to the wishes of the leaders and then we were left here to die. The leaders were merciful enough not to kill us directly since we came from the same race," explained the elderly alien.

"That's horrible," exclaimed Skyla looking at Scott.

Scott sat there thinking about everything he had heard from the Agatovian message in the bunker on Skyla's planet. He remembered that they had said they needed to destroy all Zarcovians in order to save the universe, but that just wasn't possible anymore, now that he knew there were innocent Zarcovians throughout the universe.

"Skyla, this is a problem, we can't do this mission the way we originally planned, we just can't, I mean, look out there, there are kids, families…" said Scott.

"I know, I agree. Once we get this next key, let's get back to my bunker," said Skyla.

"Yeah, I would love to get out of here, and I wouldn't mind checking in on my…" said Aegnor.

"Ahhhh, you are the key holders. I have heard stories about a device created by the Agatovians to destroy us," said the elderly alien, interrupting Aegnor.

Scott, Skyla and Aegnor looked at each other, knowing they had slipped up when they mentioned the key.

"Yes, but now that we know, we will do what we need to do to make sure your race is not hurt. Do you have the portal devices, or is that only the leaders now?" asked Scott.

"My son, yes, we have them, but they are inactive, the leaders ensured no one could leave the planet by disabling them," said the elderly alien.

"Do you think we could take one from you? We must come up with another solution to eliminate the leadership race. Skyla, I think I have an idea, but we are gonna need tools and stuff when we get back to your bunker," said Scott.

"That shouldn't be a problem," said Skyla.

"My son, I can provide you a key as requested," said the elderly alien. "Also, I think it's safe to assume you are here looking for something."

"We are looking for the third part of the key, and our map shows that it is here," said Skyla looking at her map. "Actually, it's not moving anymore and says it's right outside the hut."

They all looked up and saw a little creature sitting at the entrance of the hut, and to everyone's surprise, around its neck was the key attached to a kind of leash.

"Oh my God, that's it, that little thing has it around its neck," exclaimed Skyla.

"Ahhh, my dear, that is "Chicdraq", my grandson's pet," said the elderly alien, and clicked twice with his mouth, and the little creature came to him, almost gliding across the floor.

They all watched as the creature jumped into the elderly alien's lap, noticing 4 sets of feet under its fur, which explained why it looked like it glided so gracefully across the ground. It also explained what that movement in the brush was earlier when they were making their way down the hill, although they definitely thought the creature was a lot bigger then. It was comforting to know it was just this little thing.

"Can I see the key?" asked Skyla.

"My dear, yes, of course, you are the key holders after all," said the elderly alien and handed "Chicdraq" to Skyla.

"Oh my, Scott, it's so soft and cute. Can we get one?" chuckled Skyla and reached for the key.

Zap! Crackle! It sparked as soon as Skyla touched it. "Owww, what the? Why did it zap me?"

"Do you think it's protecting itself because it's already been activated with someone's blood?" asked Scott.

"Can you ask your grandson to come here? We think he may be a key holder," asked Skyla.

"My dear, yes, of course," said the elderly alien and yelled, "My child Kreynak!!! Can you come here, please?"

They heard the name Kreynak repeated over and over again outside the hut a few times, and then a child a little larger than Aegnor came running into the hut.

"Yes, grandpa?" said Kreynak, slightly out of breath from running from where ever he was.

"My child, can you please go to this young lady and take the key from Chicdraq," asked the elderly alien.

Scott, Skyla and Aegnor watched as Kreynak approached Chicdraq and took the key off the leash with ease.

"Oh man, I was really hoping maybe it was going to be my turn to get a key," said Aegnor feeling disappointed.

"We still have two more keys to find Aegnor, I'm sure one of them will be yours," said Scott. "Now, Kreynak, can you come to me please with the key."

Scott stood up, and as Kreynak approached with the key, his chest started to glow. The moment Kreynak was standing across from Scott with his hand up holding the key, it lifted off of Kreynak's hands and hovered in front of the Crytivat for a moment before attaching itself to the left outer points of the Crytivat and made a humming sound as it glowed even brighter. Then just like the last time with Skyla's key, as if appearing out of nowhere, a mini Crytivat now floated in front of Scott's chest.

"This is your key now, we are key holders tasked with stopping the Leader race," said Scott.

Kreynak stood there silently, bewildered and wide-eyed and reached for the key as asked, and it pricked his finger, bonding him to it. "I don't really know what's going on, but I'm in. You guys mind filling me in?"

They all laughed and explained everything that had happened so far and watched him, eyes wide with excitement. He seemed to be very enthusiastic as he kept tapping his feet, listening to them as if ready to run out of the hut and get to the next key.

Scott watched as Skyla slowly stood up and spoke, "So guys, we should get back to my bunker and sync up with the computer now that we have another key."

"Yeah, we don't have time to spare," said Scott as he got to his feet. "Hey Aegnor, you ok, man? You've been awfully quiet?"

"Yeah, yeah, um, I'm ok... Yeah, we should get moving," replied Aegnor, noticeably different from his usual demeanor.

Scott could sense something was off, and he didn't think it was just that he didn't get a key. Although that would be a big part of it, he still felt there was something else.

Scott walked to Skyla, took her hand and walked towards the elderly alien, and leaned over slightly. "Thank you for your kindness and for helping us."

"My dear, my son may you go with all the strength of the universe," said the elderly alien, then turned to Kreynak and Aegnor. "My Children, may you go with all the strength of the universe," then sat back down, having finished blessing everyone.

Scott started walking towards the exit of the hut with Skyla's hand in his, they followed Kreynak and Aegnor outside.

"Scott, can you take Aegnor when we portal, and I'll take Kreynak since he doesn't know where we are?" asked Skyla.

"No problem!!" replied Scott, "Hey Aegnor, you ready to go?"

Aegnor replied, "Yeah, let's do this. I was looking forward to a solo ride with my friend." He said it with a hint.

Scott knew something was up but knew he wouldn't get a chance to talk about it till later. They both walked together for a moment until Scott realized he didn't know exactly where they were going and shouted, "Skyla, wait, wait, are we going to say, Quastaro Noor, Bunker, Quastaro Noor Bunker…"

"Quastaro Noor!" shouted Skyla, and "Vawhoooooop" the portal appeared, and they were gone.

"I mean, seriously, that girl," said Aegnor

Scott grabbed Aegnor's hand and shouted, "Quastaro Noor!" and "Vawhooooop."

The moment Scott got to the clearing in the forest above the bunker, all he could hear was Skyla crying, and to his horror, in front of his eyes, the once beautiful city was in flames.

Made in the USA
Middletown, DE
25 November 2022

15991760R00053